Small Town Secrets

Parker Rose Mystery Series, Volume 2

Stella Mace

Published by Stella Mace, 2024.

Copyright

Also by Stella Mace

Alex Harper Mystery Series
Shrouded Deception

Mia Conrad Mystery Series
Shattered Echoes

Parker Rose Mystery Series
Small Town Shadows
Small Town Secrets

Standalone
Silence of Secrets

Chapter 1

Bang.

Parker turned her attention to the front door, which loomed at her in the encroaching darkness. Evening was settling into the salty skies; the early shadows of winter reached their tendrils across Parker's living room. An inkling of regret pounded through her veins. What gave her the bright idea to run a repair shop out of her home? It was one thing to operate as a solo agent when she was a private investigator, but now that she had expanded her business to include computer and phone restoration, customers were showing up on her stoop daily. Small-town logic prevented Parker from seeing anything wrong with that arrangement—she knew everybody, and everybody knew her. Her address was never a secret. But now, all alone with an angry fist pounding at her door, she wondered just how bright that idea was.

Bang-bang-bang.

Maybe it was the memory of Sheriff Heston that made her so afraid. She didn't use to think her neighbors were capable of heinous things. That was until the man who kept her bills paid with constant work as a private investigator and promised to safeguard the community was found guilty of murder. The sheriff's plot to somehow bring media attention and tourists to Watson Bay by killing off beloved locals in prime spaces was hackneyed—not the sort of stuff Parker expected from someone she put her faith into. He'd also endangered her, chasing her through empty alleys in the hopes of making her his next victim. Thank God Jake Squire was there to ward him off. Unfortunately, Parker was embroiled in the belief that Jake was guilty up until that very moment, just as the sheriff had intended. Though it was discovered Jake had been framed, and he and Parker were trying to make their way as friends, things were still occasionally tense.

One of the reasons she branched out into computer repair, to begin with, was so that she could lessen her relationship with the police department. They were still looking for a replacement, and that gave her an opportunity to step back a little and create space between herself and the people she was slowly beginning to distrust. Without regular assignments from the police, though, she had to make ends meet somehow. Lo and behold, Jake stepped in with all his business know-how and helped her broaden the scope of her work.

Self-employment suited her, too. She liked dictating her own schedule, even though sometimes she thought she could have benefitted from more structure. Someone breathing down her neck and telling her what to do. But she chalked that up to misery talking—a strand of self-doubt that convinced her she wasn't capable of leading a normal, busy life on her own. She didn't need her hand held just to get through the working day.

Bang-bang.

"Parker Rose?" came a voice from behind the door. It sounded muffled and masculine but not as threatening as she presumed.

With a sigh, she got up from the couch and warily looked out the peephole.

"I know you're still open," said the man.

She could hardly see him in the dying light. She decided, against her better judgment, to open up. "How can I help you?"

she asked with a forced grin. She swung the door wide—another mistake—and the man came barging in.

Before she could demand to know his identity, he whirled around, practically flinging his laptop at her in his flurry. It was Doctor Marshal, a notable practitioner in town who most everyone tried to see when they had a problem. He had a reputation for patience and compassion, but Parker wasn't getting much of that tonight. Instead, he glared at her with red eyes and a scowl fixed on his dry lips. His puckered expression aged him by a solid decade, and even when he caught himself in the throes of his anger, he didn't relax. He just stood there frozen, waiting for Parker to request to know what was wrong. When she didn't, he finally conceded.

"My laptop is broken," he muttered and waved the machine in her face.

"Okay," she replied, feeling herself unravel. At least he was just a customer with a regular problem. He was more mad at himself than he was with her. This was a standard issue. "What seems to be the problem?"

"How should I know that?"

"Um... I just mean, like, when did you start noticing it didn't work properly?"

"Today. Yesterday. I don't know."

Parker saw his arm buckle as he fatigued from holding it up. She motioned for Dr. Marshal to give it to her, but he hesitated. "I need to have a look," she offered. He didn't budge. "You know, to help you."

Dr. Marshal reluctantly handed her the device, and Parker strolled over to the coffee table. In an attempt to diffuse the situation, she pretended as though nothing was wrong: not his attitude, not her own feelings, and certainly not the ransom message that populated as soon as she turned the computer on. Patting a couch cushion for him to sit on, she smiled at Dr. Marshal until he joined her. Sinking into the sofa with a huff, he started at the blazing laptop screen forlornly.

"I almost wish the damned thing didn't turn on," he admitted.

Parker focused on the alert. A large pixelated rectangle announced in a retro font:

You can get your life back for a small fee of $15,000. I wish I were as lucky as you.

A clickable *next* button followed the message. Parker wanted to ask the doctor what it meant, but she figured he wouldn't be honest about it. She decided to be professional, refrain from prying, and just do what was asked of her.

"You have a couple options," she announced. "You can either pay the ransom, which I doubt you wanna do, or we can wipe this baby clean."

"What—" His rage had reignited, and he sat up straight.

"That being said, even if you do decide to wipe your hardware, that might not get rid of the virus. For all we know, the ransomware is installed on internal chips and could very likely repopulate once you reboot."

"So... aren't you supposed to *help* me?"

"I am."

"This doesn't sound like help; this sounds like pure laziness. *Just pay the ransom.* If it was that easy, I would've done it myself!"

"Doctor..." Parker took a deep breath, "I'm not trying to wind you up. I'm just being honest. Of all the viruses you could've caught, ransomware is easily the worst of the worst. Even getting a new computer might not solve it if the hacker finds a way to infect all the devices on your network."

"A hacker? You mean a *person* did this?"

"Well, I mean, yeah. What else?"

"I don't know... AI. *The machine.*"

Parker let a laugh slip. "A person is always behind it, Doc. What would AI gain from duping you out of money?"

He shrugged his shoulders but didn't reply. Instead, he crumpled in his seat, bringing his hands to his forehead to rub his wrinkled skin. He looked weary as if he had just come home from performing 10 surgeries in a row. Parker felt bad for the guy, wishing she could do more to help him but not wanting to get his hopes up on a futile venture. While ransomware wasn't novel, it was also above her pay grade.

"Do you remember what link you clicked on?" Parker asked in an attempt to bring him back to the present.

"What are you talking about?" His words were aggressive, but his cadence had softened. He was just a dejected man searching for answers.

"In order to get the virus, you had to have clicked something. An ad, maybe, or visited a website. Generally, these messages don't just show up on your computer one day. Unless this hacker is super advanced, maybe, but then they'd probably be asking for more than fifteen grand."

"And going after someone who actually has that kind of money," Dr. Marshal snapped. "I can't just buy a new laptop, and I certainly can't lose what's already on there. I have pictures... memories... I can't start over."

"I'm sorry, Doc."

"Please tell me there's another way. Aren't *you* a hacker? That—that's why I came to you. I can't be royally fucked like this... Pardon my French."

"I guess I could take a crack at it," Parker finally offered. She wasn't happy to do it, but then again, she was never going to improve her craft if she refused to take on challenges. The doctor was right; she did make it her job to hack into other people's devices, so why would this be any different? But she also didn't want to bear the brunt of his ire should she be unable to fix the problem entirely. "There's a chance I could access the source code of the virus and disable it that way."

"Only a chance?"

"Correct," she nodded, pleased that she had chosen her words carefully.

"You're not guaranteeing me your services, then," he scoffed.

"I don't make promises I can't keep. Like I told you, ransomware is no joke. Pretending like it's a simple process would be a lie. I'll do my best, believe me, but that may not be enough."

"I should take my business elsewhere," the doctor grumbled as he reached for the laptop.

Parker didn't swat him away, but she did say, "To who?"

He let out another defeated groan. There wasn't somewhere else for him to go. She was the only technician in town and certainly the only person he could rely upon to be discreet. Someone in a different county wouldn't owe him privacy—they'd have asked him a lot more questions about just how and where the virus came from. But Parker understood it was a source of shame and that if his reputation was spotless, something like this could mar it. He may not have been nice to her, but she figured he was just having an off day. Who wouldn't be angry in his shoes?

"Just have it ready for me in a week," Dr. Marshal demanded.

"I don't—"

"*Please*, Parker. Please. If you really wanna have a successful business and be worth a shit, you'll do it in a week."

Parker opened her mouth to retort, but the doctor was already gathering himself up off the couch and storming toward the door, still ajar. She followed after him half-heartedly, leaving his laptop open on the coffee table. The ransom note continued to blaze, even without their eyes to witness it. He had already disappeared into the dark; not even the glint of the paint on his car could be seen. She had a strange feeling like she had been accosted by a ghost. Gone before she could register—much less prove—what had happened. She locked the door behind him, thankful to be alone again but troubled by what just occurred.

His moods were torrential, shifting from second to second regardless of how or what Parker said to him. She wanted to believe he was a nice guy who had fallen on a hard time, lashing out at her solely because he wasn't used to being vulnerable and unsure. He was the person everybody went to, who trusted that they were in good hands—his hands. Of course, he didn't want to admit he had done something wrong, or stupid, or both. He didn't want Parker and the community at large to think of him as a failure in any respect. That still didn't excuse the way he spoke to her, ordering her around like she was a dog rather than someone he ought to respect.

Parker shuffled back to the living room, mulling over the conversation and failing to see where she had slipped up and deserved to have her fingers bitten off by Dr. Marshal. She couldn't identify a snide comment or malicious request but decided not to stew over the matter. She would just find herself resentful of the doctor, adding him to her list of Watson Bay members she could no longer look at the same way. Maybe that was part of his issue, too, and why he was so hostile—he didn't want to become the second pariah in just a few short months.

Could this ransomware really denote something so distasteful he had to behave in such a manner? She figured it was something lewd like pornography but expected every older man in town to occasionally partake in it. It wasn't like she was going to retrieve the exact link he followed and blast the video to the whole world.

She pulled the computer onto her lap and reread the warning a few times, wondering what would happen if she hit *next*. Surely, things couldn't get worse. The virus had already been installed, and that was the climax of the attack—anything from here on out would merely involve more taunting... right? She bit her lip as she kept her eyes glued to the screen, the ominous words burning into her retinas.

No, she should try other keys first and see what was still functional. But when she hit *command, control,* and *enter*, her fingers felt as though they were pressing down on hardened glue. Why couldn't Parker just do as she was told? Her flesh was gliding along the traction pad, and suddenly, the mouse hovered over the button. That terrible, intriguing button. Curiosity always got the better of Parker. She hit it.

The screen stayed the same, but the message shifted:

$15k is to be sent in Bitcoin to wallet address bc13lm2.

She grimaced at the standard attachment. Nothing left to see here. But the *next* button was still present. She clicked it again. This time, she'd landed on the jackpot.

You will pay for your crimes, Doctor Marshal. The depths of your evil will be made known to the public if you don't act quickly. I would ask you to choose wisely, but that would be asking too much.

She hit *next*.

Be warned, Doctor: I make good on my promises.

Chapter 2

"I've been thinking," Jake said as he tapped the plastic stirring stick against the rim of his coffee cup, "I wanna get into poetry."

Parker found it hard not to snort coffee out of her nose. The idea of Jake attempting to become a wordsmith was laughable. She pictured him with his hair splayed across his forehead like a haphazard fringe, a scarf tucked around his neck, and a small, leather-bound notebook in his hand. It was an absurd vision for a relatively straitlaced man. Despite his work as an artist, his entire collection felt overly masculine: shades of white, black, and grey; spare shapes and unfilled details; sculptures that didn't resemble anything discernible. They were all fragments of Jake's psyche and displayed the image of a talented, albeit simple, man.

"Are you getting all *inspired* by your new home?" Parker asked snidely.

Jake leaned back in his chair. "Yes, actually. It's nice being away from that loft and lofts in general. I forgot what it was like to live in a real home, with stairs that lead up to my bedroom and a backyard. It also helps that my backyard is the ocean."

"Yeah, yeah, yeah. I get it. You've got an idyllic little life going on. You somehow turned a psychopath's murderous plot into an opportunity."

"Enough with that," he chided with a roll of his eyes. "I lost things: I had to close down my gallery for the investigation. I no longer have the same amount of business. People aren't entirely convinced I'm innocent, okay? I can't just resume life as normal."

"The sheriff confessed—"

"Online forums don't care."

"Oh, come on," Parker scoffed. "Who reads and much less *believes* those?"

"I do," Jake huffed. "I'm tired of rumors always following me around, alright? That's why I left New York and came here—a place where nobody was supposed to disturb me. Now that I'm actually getting some peace and quiet, I'm finally starting to feel like myself again."

"A poet has been inside of you this whole time, just dying to get out?" Parker knew that remark would set Jake off, and yet she couldn't help herself. Despite their burgeoning friendship, Parker still enjoyed pushing his buttons, even if that meant toeing the line of their tepid tolerance for each other. She didn't want him to grow sick of her, to discard her for her bad temperament, but she also couldn't stop the words from falling out of her mouth. Something about the pucker in his gentle face endeared her.

"I don't know why I talk to you," he grumbled.

And there it was: the sentiment she knew he harbored and was always teetering on the edge of his tongue. Sometimes, she felt like she was looking for a fight, a reason to provide him an out so that when he inevitably ditches her, she'd get to be smug about it. Part of her knew their fizzled romance contributed to her peculiar behavior—she wanted to punish him for not choosing her. Or better yet, she wanted him to know how embarrassed she was to have been rejected.

Then, again, the dissolution of their could've-been romance was neither dramatic nor apparent. He could easily pull the *oblivious male* card should she bring it up and pretend as though he had no recollection of their plans for a date and her blossoming feelings for him. To Jake, Parker was just the only person who would give him the time of day, who wouldn't ogle at his misery, and who had shared part of that turbulent experience with him. Just because Parker had spent most of the investigation over the deaths in Jake's studio and apartment accusing him of being the killer didn't mean she wasn't by his side in her own messed up way.

"Probably because you don't have a knack for words," Parker retorted. She looked at him demurely, her chin pointed at the table and her eyes gazing out from under her lashes.

"Are you calling yourself an idiot?" he asked. His lips teased a soft smile.

She shrugged. "Maybe."

Parker paused to take a sip of her coffee. It was bitter and on the last legs of its mild warmth. The café, in an attempt to attract high-end customers and lost without Jake's art gallery to patronize, had overplayed their hand. They had spent all their money on décor that amounted to rickety bistro tables, as well as wall murals devoted to Paris and all things coffee. Though the downtown strip it belonged to was attempting the same upscale modernization, they were all paled by the shadow of Jake's studio.

It loomed over them from across the street. The yellow tape had all been taken down; however, the memories of violence and the promise of what could have been had Jake been able to sustain a financial endeavor for the town stared at them angrily.

Parker was thankful he wasn't still holed up there, trying to make the best of a loft space and studio riddled with ghosts.

"If I *am* calling myself an idiot," Parker continued, "will that stop you from being mad at me?"

"I'll only be mad at you if you don't come to my reading on Thursday."

Parker groaned reflexively. "Please, don't make me do that."

"Thursday at seven o'clock in Harrisburg. I'm up first, so we can't be late."

"Harrisburg?"

"Yeah, what's wrong with that?"

"You want me to have faith in your talent, and yet you don't have the balls to perform right here in Watson Bay?"

"What's that got to do with anything? Besides, it's not like there's much of a scene for poetry around here."

"If you thought you were the next Shakespeare, you'd be funding a writer's retreat and annual performance circuit, and you know it."

Jake's shoulders slumped as he picked at the stale croissant on the chipped plate before him. He hadn't taken a bite since they'd arrived 30 minutes ago. "Have you ever thought that maybe, just maybe, I want to do something for me? That I don't want to save this town? I'm allowed to have a hobby."

"It's just... one hell of a hobby."

"Well, what do you like to do in your spare time, Parker? Pick your nose? Stare at your phone? Gamble?"

"These are kindergarten-level insults, Jake," she replied with a laugh that she meant to be light and airy, but she feared it came out hostile, for his expression darkened.

"Sorry, I don't go for the throat."

A silence passed between them. Parker understood that she had taken it too far, just as she had always done, and Jake was nearing his limit.

"Anyway," he began, "I'll probably renew my lease on this rental."

"You really like it, huh?" Parker asked, relieved to be on a different subject.

"It's great. I mean, maybe it's very city-brained of me to be blown away by some nature, but I actually love waking up every morning and seeing trees, hearing birds, and nobody's honking their goddamn horn incessantly right outside my window."

"So you'll be sticking around for a while?"

He shrugged. "Guess so. I'm not on a time crunch or anything. I don't have to leave if I don't want to."

"Speaking of time crunches," Parker interjected while she downed the last of her coffee. "I got this really weird case last night."

"Oh yeah?" Jake appeared curious as he shifted positions in his chair. Now, he faced her directly.

"Yeah," Parker concurred. "Some doctor—you probably know him—Doctor Marshal, showed up like right when I was about to close and demanded I fix his laptop."

"That *is* your job."

"Duh, I know that," Parker chirped, "but that's not the weird part. He had a computer virus, standard stuff, but he refused to tell me where he got it from."

"Maybe he didn't know."

"Please. There's no excuse for that in this day and age. He either clicked on a sketchy link or was surfing a website or two that he shouldn't have been. Regardless, it wasn't just any old virus. It was asking him for a ransom—fifteen grand, to be exact. And along with the note was something strange: The hacker, whoever they are, accused him of a crime."

"What kinda crime?"

"Didn't say. The other thing is, Dr. Marshal's a really well-known guy—"

"It's hard to *not* be well-known around here."

"Exactly. Which means that the claim is either bogus—"

"Likely the case—"

"Or," Parker emphasized her interruption as she glared at Jake, who shone her a smug smile, "he's got some pretty nasty monsters buried in his closet, and it's only a matter of time before they come out. Secrets *are* possible around here, but they don't stay secrets for very long."

It was Jake's turn to shoot Parker an unenthusiastic look. "Come on, we both know it's a stretch to believe the hacker."

"I didn't say I believed them. I just think it's an odd accusation to make. Some mysterious crime the doctor wouldn't want getting out? Isn't the virus enough of a reason to pay the ransom?"

"Not really," Jake admitted. "So it's fifteen grand. He probably makes that in a month as a doctor, especially when he's sought after around these parts. He's never without business."

"That seems like an exaggeration."

"Stop." Jake waved her off. "I don't think you understand how much doctors make off private insurance. You have told me about this guy before: Gives people whatever prescriptions they want, makes referrals without hassle, provides care without judgment. These are things that would, *a,* make him money, and *b*, get him in the pocket of pharmaceutical companies and outside clinics."

"So, you're saying there *is* a chance he's scum."

"Now you're the one exaggerating. I'm just explaining the business, and frankly, I find business to be a very neutral venture."

"I can't even argue that right now. Just know I think it's an absurd thing to say."

"Whatever, Parker. You know as well as I do that this is just another instance of false blame."

He lowered himself so that his chin practically rested on his hands, which were clasped together on the table. They were the only ones in the café apart from the sole barista, who was mindlessly wiping the same patch of the countertop, her eyes staring off into blank space. Parker knew that Jake was still anxious about his reputation—he didn't like to broadcast his feelings about Sheriff Heston because he didn't want anyone to think he was still sore about it. As if being mad at his victimhood would anger the locals. He was trying to fit in, which Parker had once told him was a losing battle. She meant to encourage him to expand his travels and perhaps find a less problematic town to hole up in, but he took it as an insult. Now, he seemed determined to win everybody over like some sort of repentance. Like he was the one who needed to do the groveling.

"I don't know," Parker replied slowly, "doesn't it seem a bit far-fetched to have the same case repeat itself? There can't already be a copycat killer."

"This isn't a murder, though; it's just a computer virus. They're not comparable."

"You compared them first," Parker argued. Even though she empathized with Jake's point of view, she always sensed that he wanted her to feel bad about what she'd done. Perhaps it wasn't that he feared the town would never get over the accusations waged against him and the murders that had taken place on his property, but that he never forgave Parker. He wanted her to see him recoil, to languish in self-pity as he tiptoed around Watson Bay. He stayed because he wasn't satisfied with her apology.

"My guess?" Jake said. "Another doctor is all bitter about Marshal's success and wants to scare him away with a couple threats. Believe me, I've been on the other end of someone else's hatred and lies. Nonsense like that may not make sense to us, but guaranteed whoever's got it out for Dr. Marshal thinks this is a brilliant idea." He was nearly whispering now. Parker's desire to console Jake was giving way to her own brand of anger toward him.

"Look, I'm not saying this message isn't fake, but I also don't think this would be the right way to go about exacting petty revenge. I mean, if the police were to get ahold of the hacker, they'd be facing jail time. If doctors are swimming in money like you say, even the ones losing out to Doc Marshal wouldn't be willing to risk their lives just to steal some of his patients. A ransomware attack like this on a benign doctor in a small town simply doesn't add up. It was personalized... intentional... and I think we should be prepared to deal with the fact that Dr. Marshal may be up to no good. He doesn't have unwavering innocence just because he's a seemingly good guy."

"You vouch for his character one second and then disparage it the next. I think you're the one who wavers too much, and you know what? You shouldn't be meddling in people's lives if you can't stick to your convictions."

Parker felt herself grow red in the face. Just as she suspected, Jake's insistence that she hadn't paid her dues was interfering with his judgment. Why was he friends with her if he secretly despised her so much? Why was she friends with him if all she sought to do was atone for her sins? Sins that everybody else had moved on from but that she and Jake were still hung up over. Their relationship was becoming toxic in her mind—a bad idea that they were now stuck with. But the notion of his hatred for her sat in her stomach like a rock. She didn't want to be relieved of his anger, nor did she cling to him to feel better about herself. No, part of her liked him, and maybe that was the worst thing. She didn't just want to be forgiven; she thought maybe she wanted to be loved.

"Doctor Marshal is owed the benefit of the doubt," Jake continued, his voice getting louder the more riled up he became. "You should know better than to stick your nose in other people's business. When you're hired for a job, just do as you're asked, not as you please."

"It was my snooping that caught Sheriff Heston. Without me, he'd still be on the loose doing God knows what."

"Well, many lives were caught in the crosshairs, Parker. If you had just listened when everybody said..." He trailed off, sinking into his chair as the stiffness melted from his limbs. He was giving up the fight. He liked to beat around the bush and then drop the subject, allowing Parker's rage to take over and finish the job for him. When she snapped, that was when he won. That was when he got to continue being the victim. Sometimes, Jake was insufferable. And sometimes, Parker wondered, she was still reading him wrong because the evidence before her didn't suit her narrative. The problem was she didn't know what she wanted to believe about Jake. She never did. Just like he said, she lacked conviction.

Parker joined him in a slouch, and they both eyed each other from across the table, silent and pouting. They'd sit like this for a few more minutes until one of them gave up the game and offered to pack it in for the evening. Then, they'd go to their separate homes and not speak again until morning, when they'd resume their peculiar friendship as if nothing had happened and resentment wasn't bubbling below the surface.

This, Parker thought, was how they tortured each other.

Chapter 3

Parker was startled when Dr. Marshal banged on her door again. In spite of Jake's insistence that she give the doctor the benefit of the doubt, Parker wasn't convinced. Sure, she hadn't located anything dreadful or criminal on his laptop, but she also didn't uncover anything to exonerate him either. In fact, it appeared that Dr. Marshal was more tech-savvy than he let on, with a host of locked folders he had buried within the depths of his hard drive. In an attempt to satiate Jake, she didn't hack into the folders, though she was tempted, and decided to let sleeping dogs lie. Dr. Marshal didn't ask her to forage for clues within his personal information; he simply wanted her to deactivate the malware. Which, unfortunately, she had not been able to accomplish.

Despite regaining a modicum of access to Dr. Marshal's property, she couldn't dislodge the venomous code from his software. Every time she thought she was in, the sequence changed, and Parker was booted out. It was like pulling teeth trying to recover Dr. Marshal's hidden folders from the confines of the ransomware, and even then, she was certain the infection would consume it once again—it was only a matter of time before the hacker caught on to what Parker was doing and put a stop to it.

Parker slowly turned the knob, a blank expression across her face when Dr. Marshal came into view. He was as stoic as she was, so she motioned for him to enter her home, and he did so without a word. He scanned the interior as if regarding it for the first time and stiffly took a seat on the couch. Parker followed suit, pointing to his laptop, which rested on the coffee table in front of him.

"I can show you what I've done so far," Parker said while lifting up the screen.

"What you've done so far?" he repeated. Irritation was detectable on his tongue.

Christ, Parker grumbled internally. *So much for giving people the benefit of the doubt.*

"I expected this to be *done* done. Like fixed," Dr. Marshal continued.

"It's a very complex virus—"

"I'm sure it is," he sarcastically muttered.

"It changes as soon as I hack into it. Well, partially hack into it. It's definitely learning from my keystrokes and building up new protections. Here, let me show you," Parker offered as she booted up the computer.

"I'm not interested," he replied and sharply shut the screen. He ripped the device away from her, hastily unplugging it from the charging cable in the process, and gathered himself to leave.

"I just need some more time," Parker insisted. She followed him to the foyer, feeling suddenly desperate to keep the laptop in her possession. Doctor Marshal may have been an asshole, but the ransomware itself had become a source of intrigue for her. She didn't want to solve the case for his sake but her own.

"You've had plenty."

"Then, you're stuck with a useless laptop. There's no fixing it without me, so you're better off getting a new one and praying the virus isn't in your network."

The doctor froze at the front door, his shoulders pinched against his ears, and carefully turned around to glare at Parker. "Is that a threat, missy?"

"What?" Parker asked, stunned. "I'm just giving you the truth, Doc. You either leave it with me until I can crack the ransomware, or you get a new device."

"You know what?" the doctor sighed. "This whole thing is starting to feel like a scam."

"I'm confused—"

"Don't pretend to be some doe-eyed good girl now, Parker. I see right through your bullshit. I don't even know why I came here. You're just the local grifter who thinks she can steal money from idiot townies. Well, that's not me, kid. It's not even an intelligent grift—you're a lazy, selfish girl who wants to take the easy route to whatever your pathetic definition of success is."

"You don't mean that, Doc." Parker paled as she said the words, for she knew she was the one lying. Of course, he believed what he was saying to be true. Parker had thought those things about herself. Really, what good had she done for the community? Jake barely knew her compared to the rest of the locals, and he had her pegged as a self-serving troublemaker. All she wanted was to receive attention for resolving problems she helped to create in the first place. In a way, knowing that about herself made the doctor's accusations hurt less.

"I'm sick of everyone in Watson Bay," Doctor Marshal growled. "The lot of you—always trying to take what you think you're owed but certainly don't deserve. Now, you've resorted to installing ransomware on people's computers. You should be ashamed of yourself."

He stormed out the door, and Parker didn't chase after him. There was nothing for her to do. Nothing for her to say. She couldn't defend a person—even herself—against words, however cruel, that were laced with truth.

She shuffled back inside, nosediving into the couch as she reeled from the encounter. *Don't let this get to you.* But it would. Did she seriously think she could chase evil out of Watson Bay one petty investigation at a time? Her parents had begged her to leave when they did, but she refused to listen. She clung to the town so desperately that now, it was impossible for her to detangle herself. She had made this place her entire identity while mocking people who did the same thing. This jaded attitude of hers had gotten her nowhere—she was just a computer lackey and failing at that.

Parker knew she needed to focus her attention on fixing her broken psyche, but even after the self-flagellation, her mind went back to the code. That strange, toxic code. This was why she would never muster up the courage to leave; she couldn't put her talents in the right place. Before she could make an honest, substantial change, Parker knew she had to dissolve the malware even if Doctor Marshal didn't want her to.

***

"Dr. Marshal came by again," Parker announced.

Jake handed her a mug of tea, which he made from herbs he'd crushed and bagged himself, and proudly presented it to her. When she asked if this was another hobby of his, he grimaced, insisting he'd always been particular about his tea and found that making it himself simply tasted better. Once again, Parker was the asshole.

She probably should have canceled her plans with Jake after her altercation with Doctor Marshal, knowing she'd be grumpy and looking to take her anger out on somebody. But she wanted to see him. He was an itch she couldn't scratch, and even when they were bickering, she still managed to be sated by his company. She was sure her growing allure would blow up in her face, especially when it was embroiled in rage and resentment the pair were building against each other, but that was a problem for another time. Right now, Parker was perched on Jake's leather couch, a knitted blanket atop her lap and rain pelting against the broad windows. Outside, the skies had turned gray, the waters became unsettled, and winds whipped ocean spray across the beach below them. Jake was settling in beside Parker, pulling a corner of the blanket over his thigh.

"Oh yeah?" Jake asked, pretending not to be slightly amused by the information.

"And he was a real jerk to me."

"I'm sure he was."

"Seriously, Jake," Parker grumbled. She took a sip of her drink, wincing as the delicious warmth cascaded down her throat. Damn, that *was* some good tea. Perhaps she could goad him into learning how to cook, too. Homemade meals and tea? Jake was a dream man. Somebody else's idea of a dream man, of course. Parker couldn't let herself get caught up in his potential.

"Fine," he sighed. "Tell me. But your story can't take more than twenty minutes. Our pizza is on the way. You know," he began, attempting to change the subject, "West Coast pizza is a lot different from the East Coast."

"Let me guess: The East's is better?"

"Always. We invented it. You West Coasters put things like french fries on there, and like your crust gooey and thick. It's weird."

"Why do you even bother ordering it?"

Jake gave a cavalier shrug. "Old habits die hard, I guess."

"Or maybe we're doomed to keep making the same mistakes, knowing the consequences."

"That's another way to look at it. If you're a teenage goth girl, that is."

"Back to the main issue," Parker interjected, glowering at Jake until he conceded. She knew he was stalling in an attempt to keep the peace, but it wasn't possible. Nothing was ever civil for long between them. "So, Dr. Marshal shows up and once again wails on my door like I can't hear him."

"Go on," he half-heartedly urged.

"And look, I haven't been able to terminate this virus. I didn't veer off course, I didn't make new problems or whatever else you wanna accuse me of, but I did try my hardest. But the code altered every time I looked at it. Like, the lines scrambled themselves the second I hacked into the virus. So, figuring out how to actually disable it became a nightmare, and Doc Marshal, as impatient as he is, barged in before I could finish."

"Did he call first?"

Parker scowled. "Of course, not. He didn't give me a due date or anything, either. He just showed up and expected it to be done. When I tried to explain to him how complex it was, he went off on me. And get this: He said *I'm* the one who put that ransomware there. Granted, he also called me pathetic, a liar, a deadbeat, blah blah blah... but holding him for ransom? That's ridiculous!"

Jake pursed his lips as he carefully thought about his reply, which to Parker was a bad sign. "So, you both have reservations about each other."

"Ugh!" Parker flung her head back and stared at the ceiling.

"It's not right, sure, but it's kinda fair."

"Just because I questioned him just a little bit—and in *private*, mind you—doesn't mean he gets to accuse me of trying to steal money from him."

"What do you want me to say, Parker?" Jake commanded her attention with his tormented cadence.

"That this is fucked up. That Doc Marshal shouldn't be treating me this way."

"Well—"

"That he's *wrong*. I mean, Jesus, Jake, why do you hang out with me if you think I'm the devil?"

"Hey, I never said that."

"Look, I have groveled and begged and pleaded with you to forgive me," Parker started. She wouldn't be able to stop now that she'd opened the floodgates. It wasn't her nature to put her foot in her mouth. "I thought you were the killer for a while there, yes. But can you blame me? You were a stranger! The murders were taking place in your apartment! I saw a dead body in the middle of the room, and then you chased after me! I was just trying to protect myself, not enact some petty revenge against you like the sheriff. Why do you insist on seeing me as his sidekick or something? Like I had something to do with what happened to you?"

"Because you did, Parker. You helped spread the narrative that I was the killer."

"I kept that shit to myself! Same as I'm doing now! You're the only person I've mentioned my misgivings about Doc Marshal to. Nobody even knows about his ransomware attack. The world isn't watching us, Jake. I don't know what to do to make you believe that."

"It's not about eyes being on us, it's... it's the fact that you're willing to protect some crook messing with somebody's laptop. Regardless of how you feel about Dr. Marshal, he's your client—your friend, even—not your enemy."

"Now, who's simplifying things? People aren't always good, and they're not always bad. And just because someone's kind to the public doesn't mean they're not a shitty person behind closed doors. What's so out there about that, huh? Isn't that just human nature?"

"It's human nature to do a lot of things. I'm not interested in the condition of man or whatever. I'm just asking you to be nicer to the people around you, okay? Stop trying to make monsters where there aren't any."

"But we do have monsters in Watson Bay. For all your anger, Jake, you've never taken it out on Sheriff Heston. Just me. He's let off the hook despite what he did, but I have to keep taking the heat? I never laid my hands on anybody; at least I have that."

"We're getting nowhere with this," Jake grudgingly announced, holding up his hands in an effort to silence Parker.

She tensed her body, gathering all the venom she could to spew at him, but she lost steam somewhere between her brain and her mouth. Something about Jake's big eyes disarmed her.

Once again, she was caught in a tug-of-war between her mind and heart. If she were any wiser, she would have left him alone. It wasn't fair to either of them to keep on with their verbal sparring while they quietly sorted out their feelings for each other in the background.

"Let's just... agree to disagree," Parker offered.

"Fine," he uttered. "Pizza's almost here, anyway."

"I get to pick the movie this time," she said, grabbing the remote.

They both zoned out as the TV came to life, and Parker sifted through his channels, hoping the mindless act would soften her. Instead, her ire piled up inside, stacking itself atop her bones and muscles, aching to break free. Jake was hellbent on preventing her from digging around in people's dirt, and perhaps that was because there was something he had to hide, too. Sure, it wouldn't be gnarly like murder and ransom, but he wasn't exactly forthcoming about his own agenda. What did it matter to him what Parker thought of the local doctor? If her moral compass was truly askew, why was he glomming onto her, anyway?

She wanted to ask him these things, to get to the bottom of his fascination with her. She had her own theories, but he was too old to be cozying up to the mean girl who decided she'd retract her fangs for a while. He was up to something, just like everybody else in this world; he just didn't want to admit it. He reveled in the self-righteousness he got to adopt since beating a murder charge, but that couldn't carry him forever. He'd have to reveal himself when the dust finally settled, and he was no longer the new, eccentric, and handsome artist in town, who also happened to be the victim of Watson Bay's first scandal.

Jake placed the pizza box on the coffee table and brought over shakers of red pepper flakes, garlic salt, and parmesan cheese.

"Humor me and do up your slice," he said, referring to his collection of toppings.

"Okay, Mr. New York," Parker obliged.

They ate their pizza in silence.

Chapter 4

"I need to see Dr. Ang," Parker announced into the receiver.

"What for?" asked the surly receptionist.

"Stomachache."

"Take any over-the-counter medications for it?"

"No... I mean, yes. They just didn't work."

She could hear the lady on the other end rolling her eyes as she scoured through Dr. Ang's timesheets. Parker knew there would be availability—unless the entire population of Watson Bay was sick at the same time, Dr. Ang had no reason to be jam-packed with visitors. This town wasn't the kind of place that had overrun emergency rooms and hospitals that couldn't keep up. Hell, even the police were looking for something to do most days, and thankfully, they stopped resorting to lowbrow traffic tickets. The receptionist was just trying to get out of booking an appointment for Parker. Two clicks were too much of a hassle, apparently.

God, I'm becoming my parents, Parker thought with a grimace.

"If this is a medical emergency, ma'am, Dr. Ang can't help you," she said after a while.

"It's not an emergency; I can hold out for a few more days," Parker replied.

It wasn't a lie, either. Her stomach had been killing her. Mostly with disgust and shame, as she rifled through private documents trying to amass dirt on Dr. Marshal. Despite no longer being in possession of his laptop, effectively ending her experiments with the ransomware code, Parker wasn't done with the case. She decided to keep her trap shut and leave Jake out of it. She didn't want another monologue about how terrible of a person she was and how unable she was to follow orders. Orders from who? She was working for herself now, and she preferred it that way. There was no deadline by which she needed to acquire the right piece of intel about Dr. Marshal—she could peruse at her own pace.

However, she wasn't exactly swimming in evidence. Despite mining several databases, Parker wasn't sure what she was looking for. Either there was nothing of note about Dr. Marshal, rendering the ransom a ploy to eek some money out of the doctor at random, or he was so deeply in the pockets of this town that nobody wanted to cop to his criminality.

She opted to begin with the hospital, scouring their death records for anything suspicious, such as bills generated by the doctor that seemed inflated or inconsistent, but to her uneducated eye, everything was in order. She considered accessing Dr. Marshal's personal computer located at the clinic but decided that was going a bit too far. Regardless of her continued effort to blame him for something or exonerate him entirely, she couldn't cross that boundary. She always tried to keep her hacking to the realm of the impersonal: institutions, businesses, and dangerous strangers. Just because Doc Marshal would never know the level of snooping she'd gotten up to with his documents didn't mean she would feel good about it.

Sometimes, though, she wondered if she had the balls to wage a proper investigation. Was she really falling back on her sense of right and wrong, or was she too scared to really commit to a project? She kept her private investigating to a minimum, but maybe if she got down and dirty, she'd be able to incorporate and build a proper business. Ethics didn't really have a place in her field, especially if she wanted to be genuinely good at it. For all her snark, her bark didn't really have a bite, and that only contributed to her feelings of worthlessness. Why was she constantly holding herself back?

Parker keeled over, a stomach cramp radiating through her intestines as she gripped the phone tightly to her ear. She inhaled sharply, and the receptionist, who continued to play with her keyboard instead of logging anything into her computer, gasped at the sound.

"I really think you should go to the emergency room," she repeated.

"No, goddammit, I need to see Dr. Ang," Parker snapped. "I have other questions for her, too, alright?"

"Like what?"

"Whatever happened to doctor-patient confidentiality?"

Doctor Marshal was clean with the IRS, too, and never made a withdrawal from the bank larger than a few grand. Nothing dubious, especially when she considered all the lump payments adults had to make for things like houses and cars. She winced at the idea of othering herself from adulthood—she was getting closer to 30 every day. She'd have to stop coddling herself at some point.

The police department didn't even have Doctor Marshal's name in their system—he'd never so much as sped through a residential neighborhood or rolled a stop sign. Even when Parker searched for general complaints about the hospital, the clinic, and all the practitioners, Dr. Marshal had nothing but rave reviews from his patients. They didn't seem to be generated by bots, nor were they so dramatic as to raise alarms.

He was just a normal man doing his job. And yet, Parker still wasn't convinced. What would it take for her to give up the game?

The angrier with herself she became, the more her stomach pulsated in agony. The pain started as a story, though—she'd crafted an excuse to delve deeper into her constructed narrative. She had to speak with a colleague of Dr. Marshal's, someone who knew the ins and outs of the system and could point her toward anything questionable. Dr. Ang was always easy to get along with and utterly fascinated by Parker's profession. Of course, she wouldn't stroll in there with an announcement about her doubts in regards to Dr. Marshal's character—she'd wrap her queries up with neat little bows and hard-to-discern motives—but she didn't doubt that Dr. Ang would play ball in some capacity.

However, the more she seesawed over her ideas and accusations, the more the pain in her stomach evolved into something entirely real and entirely nasty. Parker was about to bite the bullet and switch doctors if it meant being seen—maybe she could even worm her way into Dr. Marshal's office, but that didn't seem like an intelligent move. Just because she was impatient didn't mean she had to implode her whole investigation—if you could call it that.

"Alright, the doctor will see you tomorrow at two in the afternoon. Does that work?" the receptionist offered.

"Perfect. Thanks."

***

Parker was restless as she sat on the waiting room chair. It was easily a couple of decades old and riddled with stains that Parker feared resulted from one too many bathroom accidents. The place hadn't changed at all—Parker had been visiting with Dr. Ang since she was a kid and never found a reason to branch out. Who shopped around for doctors? She wasn't one to insist upon contracting diseases and illnesses and was determined to fix pretty much any problem she had on her own. She was quite pleased with herself when she found the right concoctions to drive away a sore throat or a rash.

The office, however, remained a relic of the past. There was an assortment of built-in shelves full of dusty magazines dated back at least 20 years, the walls were a faded pink, and the artworks were all pencil drawings of dogs and sailboats. The receptionist's desk was hidden behind a pane of frosted glass, which she had to push with all her might to open. It scraped against the desk when Parker arrived, and the lady frowned at her while she handed her a clipboard with some basic questions to answer.

Dr. Ang was already a half hour late, and Parker was dying to start gathering research. Armed with her sheets filled out, she knocked on the glass, and the receptionist greeted her with that same scowl.

"All done," Parker proclaimed. She pushed the clipboard over to her, and the receptionist took it wordlessly. "You guys are still busy, huh?"

The receptionist peered out at the empty waiting room. Parker was the only occupant. "You betcha," she concurred lamely.

"I bet things can get pretty boring around here," Parker continued.

The lady shrugged. "No more boring than anything else."

Her jowls wobbled as she spoke, the excess skin touching the beaded necklace attached to her glasses. Parker caught a whiff of her hairspray, which coated her bleached strands until they were hardened and crunchy, and she fought back disgust. The woman smelled like the discounted perfume aisle at a drugstore. She wore a plain T-shirt and gaudy gem bracelets and was outfitted with a headset. Her name was nowhere to be found—evidently, she didn't want to consort with patients. Parker had to schmooze a lot harder if she wanted to get anywhere.

"Tons of gossip, too, I bet," Parker chimed. "Shame there's no one to gab about it with."

This time, the receptionist simply didn't respond at all.

"Like, what happens when a patient gets out of control? Has a full-blown meltdown?"

"We call security," the lady said plainly.

"Does it happen often?"

"I don't know."

"When was the last time?"

"I don't know."

"Do you and Dr. Ang talk about the other doctors? You know, the fussy ones who don't like to take appointments or the ones who get caught overprescribing stuff?"

Nothing.

"What about the nurses? Do you guys have to deal with them a lot? Like, when you have to work out of the hospital instead of the clinic? Like, if a patient is giving birth, or something."

"Dr. Ang stopped working in the delivery room when she turned forty."

"Oh... how come?"

The receptionist glared at Parker. "Please sit down, ma'am. The doctor will be with you shortly."

"Okay..." Parker replied awkwardly. She stepped back without taking her eyes off the receptionist, who was already preparing to shut her little window. "If you want to talk at all, I'm here. Maybe I'm the one who's bored." She forced out a bright chuckle.

When it was obvious the receptionist wasn't going to change her mind, though, Parker retreated. Taking up her seat, she tapped her anxious toes on the carpet.

***

Parker swung her legs like a child while she continued her wait for Dr. Ang. She had finally been let into the exam room, but now she was perched on the paper-lined bed, staring at the form of a skeleton across the room. The interior was no less dull and dated, and Parker was beginning to lose steam in the middle of her mission. Something about the atmosphere was weighing her down, and her stomach had settled enough to ease her mind. Perhaps she should just go through with the pleasantries and call it a day.

"Hello, Miss Rose," Dr. Ang cooed as she strolled through the door.

She was still the same delightful woman, and that brought Parker a modicum of peace. Her black hair was frizzy at the ends despite her straight texture, her glasses were a bit too big for her face, and her professional trousers poked out from under the length of her white coat. She always wore the same three shades of brown. Her lotion was scented like fresh cotton, and her hands were always drenched with the stuff. She kept an extra bottle at her desk and routinely applied it—a habit she couldn't break.

"Long time no see," added Dr. Ang. She sat down at her computer and swiveled the chair until she faced Parker.

"Yeah, it's been a while," Parker agreed.

"You know, you should come in for a checkup at least once a year."

"Ah, I think I'm fine."

"Your stomach?"

"For the most part, then," Parked said sheepishly.

"Tell me, what brought it on? Do you know?"

"I've been eating a lot of takeout lately. Maybe that's it?"

"Did you stop once you noticed the pain was persistent?"

"Yeah."

"Okay, so then perhaps not that. What else? Do you have a lot of gas?"

"Not really. I don't drink or smoke either, really, if that's what you were gonna ask next."

"I was," she replied with a smile. "Any medications?"

"Nope."

"Hm. I see. That job of yours can be pretty stressful, eh?"

"Yeah. But I haven't been doing much of it. I haven't been doing much of anything."

"Well, that doesn't mean you're not stressed just because you're not up to much."

"You think that's it? Just some stress?"

"Stress, anxiety... they have terrible consequences for the body."

"You must deal with that all the time," Parker replied, attempting to draw Dr. Ang into the conversation she came here for. Something about the mention of her daily stressors made her twitch, and she felt her usual indignation creeping in again.

"Oh, not terribly," the doctor admitted.

"Really?"

"Yes, I guess so. How are your relationships? Have any luck finding a boyfriend?"

"Eh, I have a weird thing with this one guy."

"Ah, another source of anxiety. Have you thought about seeing a therapist?"

"Do you go to one?"

Dr. Ang blushed. "No, no... In my youth, a little bit. But I think we all need someone to talk to sometimes. I don't regret it, but I'm certainly more levelheaded now and don't need it."

"But you must have crazy patients. And the other doctors... I bet they're difficult to get along with."

"What makes you say that?" She pursed her lips but didn't appear offended by the remark.

"I mean, this must be an exhausting profession, helping people with their problems and all. Seeing people die. That kinda stuff."

"That happens a lot less often than you think." She turned in her chair and clicked her computer screen. "Now, I'm going to prescribe you some antacids. They'll help you regulate the stomach pain for a while, but they aren't anything extreme. The stuff you can buy at the grocery store is pretty good, too, and I recommend taking those if this problem occurs again. Or, Parker, consider finding an outlet for all that stress. It'll do you good. My preference is yoga. My daughter and I go every week to this little... hm. This is annoying."

Parker perked up. Admittedly, she'd stopped listening once Dr. Ang had changed the subject, attempting to refocus it on Parker and her myriad of problems. "What?" she asked nosily.

"I've been having trouble with these darned computers all day. Now they won't even let me pull up the internet." She tapped the mouse repeatedly. "Your file is all blotchy, too. And the cursor is jumping around..." She pulled out her phone and logged in. "Perhaps I can do something with this. I'm not good with all this technology, but I've been told they're synced, somehow."

Parker craned her neck, watching as the doctor struggled to operate her device. "Corrupted, too?"

"Unfortunately."

"You mind if I take a look?" Parker held out her palm.

Dr. Ang hesitated; a sigh caught in her throat, but she eventually relented. "It's not exactly protocol to allow a patient to open up her own file, but you make a living helping us technologically inept folks fix our machines."

Parker eagerly swiped through the doctor's phone, perusing her various apps quickly and noting nothing out of place for a woman in her middle age. "What am I looking for?" Parker asked, but then the phone froze. She frowned.

"Well, I don't know," said Dr. Ang.

"You said your phone and computer are synced? Like, they're on the same network?"

"Same account. I upload things to the *cloud*. Or so my daughter tells me," she added with a frivolous laugh. She seemed in good spirits for someone struggling to perform basic functions in her daily work.

Parker looked back down at the phone screen, and something strange appeared:

You can get your life back for a small fee of $15,000. I wish I were as lucky as you.

Chapter 5

Parker stared at the glowing phone like it was a trophy. While she couldn't take Dr. Ang's computer home with her, she was granted access to her cellular, and boy, was Parker psyched. It was the exact same ransomware as the one infecting Dr. Marshal's device, but this time, the afflicted was not dodging Parker's questions.

"Do you remember when this started?" Parker had asked.

Dr. Ang puzzled out the details for a moment before replying. "You know what? Now that I think of it, I got a weird text message not too long ago. They claimed they were my bank, and it was one of those four- or five-digit numbers that pop up when you're getting a message from a company or something. So I thought it was real. The text said I had gone over my account limit or whatever, and I thought that was strange since I'm pretty meticulous about my spending, how much is in my accounts, and so on.

"Well, I followed the link, and it sort of looked like my banking page. There were a few inaccuracies in the font size, but I didn't really pay much mind to it until after I'd punched in a bunch of information. But, once I realized there was something fishy going on, I closed out of the browser."

"That was it?" Parker inquired.

"I thought so. I went to my bank the next day—*in person*—and none of my accounts had been messed with. Money was all there, security information was intact, and everything was all fine. Just a false alarm. Well, I believed that at the time. But now this—" She gestured to the phone.

"The hacker must have installed the virus when you clicked the link," Parker informed Dr. Ang. "That's usually how these things work."

"But why didn't they just take my money?"

"Huh?"

"They likely had access to my funds the moment I started inputting all my criteria, no? Now they want money for control over my phone and computer again. Yet they lured me in with a financial scam... I just don't get it."

Parker glanced at the message emblazoned on the screen:

$15k is to be sent in Bitcoin to wallet address bc13lm2.

"They want Bitcoin," Parker told her. She watched the bafflement creep up on the doctor's features. "It's a type of cryptocurrency. It's basically untraceable—not connected to a traditional bank account or wire transfer number. For a hacker looking to make away with a lot of money, it's smarter to go this route. Less people will be able to find the source of the claim."

"But you can, right?" Dr. Ang looked at Parker expectantly.

"I'll try, that's for damn sure."

And so here Parker was, curled up on the couch with Dr. Ang's phone searing her skin. She wasn't sure where to start, but the device was burning with potential. She had clicked through the hacker's message, and it was the same one that had been sent to Dr. Marshal, word for word, including the accusation of some grievous crime. The lack of personalization was a win for Dr. Marshal—it was a lot harder to believe, even for Parker, that two local doctors were part of some ring of cruelty that warranted being held hostage.

However, the repeated message didn't exactly make for a direct route to an answer. While she promised Dr. Ang she would try to follow the Bitcoin username, she was fairly certain it would lead to another dead end. It wasn't likely to be an apt use of her time to entertain such futile matters. Dr. Ang may have been grateful now, but Parker was well aware that things could change drastically, and she'd have yet another piece of the puzzle ripped from her hands in a matter of days. If only there was something concrete for her to latch onto.

She booted up her laptop with the intention of accessing Dr. Ang's phone from an outside source. If there was a discernible route the hacker had followed, perhaps she'd be directed to a beginning or an end point. Unsurprisingly, the doctor's software was malleable due to its connection to data clouds. Something as small as her AirDrop function was an attack point for Parker, and with only a few swift keystrokes, she was within the internal system.

"Nice," she whispered to herself.

But victory didn't last long in Parker's household. The hacker somehow foresaw another individual trying to access already infected devices, and blockades began cropping up on Parker's computer. She closed out of the first window relatively quickly, but as she moved her mouse across the tracker pad, the malware picked up on her presence and sent another irritating window her way. The more she engaged with them, the more they appeared, swarming her computer until the entire screen was a wall of taunting messages from the assailant.

Better luck next time, they read. *Don't make me raise the stakes.*

"If I could just shut my mind off..." Parker grumbled to herself as she sifted through the intense barrage.

The noise each window made as it appeared was grating her nerves. She felt her teeth clenching and her jaw contracting, sending ripples of pain throughout her mouth as she puckered and fought. The onslaught would not relent. Even as she opened new tabs to write lines of code that would implement an order to force a ceasefire, her fingers failed to type as quickly as the hacker's pop-ups appeared. She was engaged in a losing battle.

Grunting, she powered down her laptop and shut the screen, unable to witness her mounting failures anymore. Why were these doctors so important to the hacker? Who would be willing to spend this much time building an intricate net of viruses in order to prevent anyone from disabling the original ransomware? The attacker's hatred must have been vast and, though potentially misplaced, had to mean something. Parker certainly wouldn't put her mind to such uses for no gain, and she couldn't expect any hacker to be this determined to scam a few random doctors out of cash. So what gives?

Just as frustrated with her own inability to pick a side, Parker couldn't let her work fall to the wayside for the evening. Not again. She had to find something, and if she was truly unable to paint a small picture of this hacker, then she had best give up her status as a tech nerd and return Dr. Ang's devices. She was doing nobody any good, especially not herself.

Refocusing on Dr. Ang's phone, Parker investigated the device's analytics and hosting logs. Naturally, the hacker had managed to hide their access to Dr. Ang's software, but Parker had a few tricks of her own up her sleeve. Typing in several different commands, Parker sent a trace route onto all systems utilizing the cellphone. She scoured every possible avenue, from email to Dr. Ang's website and internet account. Every time a source bounced back, Parker simply tried again. It was a process of elimination, as well as the dumb hope that she would eventually wear *something* down: the hacker, the malware, or the tracing commands. Something had to give.

The phone *pinged* with an alert. Parker gasped. Finally, after hours of undisrupted work, she was staring at the hacker's IP address.

***

"You got 'em?" Jake asked. He sat on the edge of the couch, nervously playing with his fingers in his lap. The pair hadn't exactly spoken since their last blowout fight, but Parker didn't have anyone else to share the news with. For all his moaning and groaning, Jake was still invested in her journey. Better yet, he hadn't found anyone to replace her company with. When she called, he answered.

"Yup," Parker replied with an enthusiastic nod.

"Holy shit," Jake said in a half-whisper. "So... who is it?"

"Oh, well, that I don't know."

"Huh?"

"I found the IP address."

"Okay... that's not exactly, like, a real address. You know that, right?"

"Of course I do," Parker sighed while playfully shoving Jake. He looked at her with coy confusion.

"Then... what *do* you know?"

"The IP address."

"Parker—"

"I already searched the location, and it's a legitimate house in the next town over, alright? Doesn't look like anything much, and strangely, who owns it isn't public record. I did manage to unearth a name attached to it somewhere deep in a newspaper article from like two decades ago, and the story wasn't even about the people who lived there. I think they gave the reporter a fake name: the Bensons. Dave and Martha Benson have no arrests, fingerprints, accomplishments, businesses, or even birth certificates.

"Now, you might be wondering, *But Parker, what if they were born in a different country?* And I think that's a fair question, so I broadened my search and still got fuck all. I mean, don't get me wrong, there are a bunch of Bensons in the world, but I think that's why our hacker went for that name to begin with: basic and unassuming and easy to mask."

"Does this mean there's two of 'em?" Jake inquired.

Parker shrugged. "Maybe? I don't know. A couple who steals together stays together, I guess. But also, if we're following the timeline of that news article, they have to be in their sixties by now, so why they're wasting their retirement years committing online thievery is a bit odd."

Jake shook his head. "Maybe they got fucked out of their pensions somehow. Maybe one or both of them used to work in healthcare, and with the new slate of doctors coming onto the scene, something in their contracts got changed. They feel like they've been gypped, so they're taking it out on anybody and everybody they deem even remotely related to it."

Parker sank into the couch cushions, beaming at Jake. "Good investigative work, Mr. Squire."

"Please…" he murmured. He corrected himself shortly after, "That doesn't mean I'm blaming Dr. Ang and Marshal and stuff. They could still be innocent—collateral damage is all."

"I know that," Parker replied. "You don't have to be pointing fingers in order to do good work, Jake."

"You should tell yourself that sometime."

Parker practically popped a vein, listening to Jake lay into her again. No matter how many months had passed or how quiet she had been, he was still seething in the background, waiting for an opportunity to exact his revenge. This time, however, she wouldn't acknowledge it. There was no point in engaging in another endless argument over who had the moral high ground in any and all situations just because Parker had made an incorrect initial judgment about him.

"I'm gonna go look at the house tomorrow," Parker announced.

"What?" He seemed genuinely troubled by her declaration. "You'll get caught. They could be dangerous people."

"Calm down," she chided. "Like I said, they're probably elderly and brittle. I can take 'em. Besides, I'll be going at night to stake it out, not rifling through their trash and banging on doors."

"You're not gonna go talk to them?"

"Not yet. I have to do my research first. I can't just barge into a war zone and expect it to go my way. I don't even know who to pretend to be or what leading questions to ask to get them to reveal their secrets to me. The satellite images of the street are pretty bleak, too—lots of abandoned houses."

"Alright, I guess that makes sense. Nobody really comes around, so why would a stranger be on their doorstep out of the blue like that."

"Exactly."

"But how do you expect to gather intel from inside your car?"

"Binoculars, plant a wire on them, creep around the windows when they're asleep—shit like that."

"That sounds fine in theory, but... this is a wholly unpredictable situation."

"Yeah, I'm aware."

"So you shouldn't go alone."

"And why not?" Parker folded her arms across her chest indignantly, but her mind was alight with the potential of Jake joining her. He'd have her in close enough quarters to needle her, sure, but perhaps the ice would finally start to melt once he spent quality time with her at a location that wasn't either of their homes.

"Because it's not safe," he insisted.

"I'll be fine." Parker wasn't trying to persuade him out of coming. In fact, she wanted him to beg for it. She wanted to hear just how much he was dying to throw himself in front of a smoking gun for her. The prospect of Jake thirsting to protect her made her silently wish for a genuine threat tomorrow.

"I don't want to see you get hurt. If I hadn't been there last time... the sheriff could've killed you."

Parker brought her hand to her throat, remembering the sensation of the violent act. Suddenly, the idea of being in the midst of danger wasn't as compelling, even with Jake by her side.

"I'll come with you, okay?" Jake offered.

"Okay," Parker replied.

Chapter 6

Crickets hummed as Parker and Jake pulled up outside the hacker's home. They were only 20 minutes beyond Watson Bay's limits in a town called Thorton, but the entire drive over had been a desolate one. They cruised through country highways, where the only light that paved their way shone down on them from the sky. They took Jake's car, which wasn't outfitted for such a barren landscape—his headlights barely penetrated the darkness, leaving them to uneasily peer into the shadows, hoping to spot any deer before they jumped out of the brush and in front of his bumper.

When the town finally cropped up amongst the vast farmland, it was similarly empty. Houses were abandoned, the boarded-up windows decaying in the damp atmosphere. Asphalt was cracked, with weeds sprouting from the breaks. The air smelled of nothing—not gasoline, salt, or vegetation. The silence, the emptiness, it felt oppressive.

"Who would want to live out here?" Parker whispered.

"Maybe it was nice once," Jake offered. "Quaint."

"It's strange that I don't recognize this place. Makes me feel unsettled."

"How come? This isn't your town."

"Yeah, but it's my county."

"So?"

"You grew up in a big place, Jake. You think it's normal to not know every square inch of your hometown. I bet there are parts of New York you've never even been to."

He tried to deny the claim, but all he did was sputter in the absence of words.

"All of this should at least be *sort of* familiar to me," Parker added.

Jake turned off the car, the whirring of the engine sounding like a concert amidst the stillness. They both twisted their necks to look at the house, which sat in the middle of a mostly vacated neighborhood. The windows did not reveal what was inside, for the home was filled with darkness. The siding was a white aluminum, which appeared relatively clean, and the front lawn, albeit small, was not yet overgrown. There wasn't a car in the lot, but a few trucks were parked further up the road, with a few stowed on driveways.

"You think that's them?" Jake asked, nodding in the direction of the other vehicles.

"No, that doesn't make sense," Parker replied. "Why would they park all the way up there when they basically have free rein over the outside of their property? And they have a driveway."

Jake shrugged. "People do strange things. Maybe they want to establish dominance over the block."

"Come on..."

"They're hackers."

Some of the tension let up as Parker processed his statement. "So am I, Jake, and I'm not like trying to run a whole street. Scare people away with my car."

"I don't know. Americans love their cars; assign them personalities and stuff."

"Are you stalling?"

"No," he muttered.

"It'll be fine," Parker said, unsure if she believed her words to be true. "Besides, maybe this is the best-case scenario. Any sound we hear, we'll just assume it's the hackers, and we'll run away."

"They'll see us before we get very far, though. There's nothing to really cover our tracks."

Parker unlocked the door, and Jake grabbed her arm on reflex. "Where are you going?" His tone was laced with worry.

"To investigate," Parker said dramatically. "We can't do that from inside the car."

"What? I thought you said you'd be looking at 'em with binoculars."

"I lied a little."

"Parker—"

"But nobody's home! So it's no big deal. Besides, I think I did mention peeping in windows, so I don't see how you could be shocked right now." She yanked her arm out of his clutches and looked both ways before darting across the street.

Jake grumbled while he got out of the car, leaving his door slightly ajar to give himself a head start in case somebody showed up. Parker was already on the front stoop, gazing at the door knob as if her eyes could detect fingerprints and carefully lifting the lid of the mailbox to inspect its contents.

"Parker!" Jake hissed, running up behind her.

But she was too fast. Sprinting along the side of the house, she ducked below windowsills, waiting until just the right moment before popping her head up and peering inside. Even up close, it was still too dark to make sense of the interior. The blinds weren't drawn, but nothing illuminated the size and shape of the furniture. Perhaps it was a barren space, and that was why she couldn't see anything. There was nothing there to look at.

"I think the place is empty," she whispered to Jake, who had finally caught up.

He leaned against the side of the building, struggling to conceal the shrill noise of his panting. "Well, that's good, isn't it?"

"Not really. I mean, good for right now since there's nobody to catch us or even care that we're poking around out here. But bad for business. At some point, I'm gonna need a name."

They went around to the back door. Jake tripped over a garbage bag, many of which had been strewn about the property. He jumped, startled by the noise he had made, and just as quickly tried to conceal his comedic fear. Parker stifled a giggle as she watched the panic swell on his features, wondering how he managed to live in a crime-ridden big city but now couldn't stomach a little bit of mischief.

Parker crept up to the door and pushed her forehead against the glass, forcing her eyes to make sense of the dark. Shadows swirled as her vision adjusted, and with a bit of extra light streaming in from the moon, Parker could identify a few cardboard boxes scattered along the floor and a couple of large pieces of furniture arranged in one of the front rooms.

"See anything?" Jake asked nervously.

"I dunno. Maybe a few signs of life." She twisted the knob, and the lock unlatched.

"What?" Jake was getting too antsy for the mission.

She pulled the door open and looked back at him with a foolish grin on her face. "Nice!" she whispered loudly.

"You can't go in there!"

"Why not?"

"Because... because it's illegal!"

Parker rolled her eyes and plunged into the home. She tucked herself against the wall, covering her back as if she were an agent entering an armed killer's house. She almost took pleasure in reliving her own chase, for this time, she had the upper hand. She knew who the murderer was before he could get to her. She was tempted to hold her hands together like a gun, but she wouldn't be able to live that down if Jake caught sight of her. No, she had to remain cool, especially with him so riled up and embarrassed by his behavior.

"Please, come back here, Parker," Jake pleaded. He hovered over the threshold, unable to take the leap.

The beckon of his voice distracted her, and Parker accidentally banged against a countertop.

"Don't touch anything, either," he warned.

This outburst caused Parker to stub her toe against the wall. "Jake!" she spat. "Enough!" She moved deeper into the home, revealing what her eyes had landed upon earlier: a large sofa positioned to face the fireplace, and a coffee table against the furthest wall. "You're either with me, or you're not," she continued.

"You should have worn quieter shoes. I can hear you from all the way over here!"

"Jake, seriously—"

"Or at least pick your feet up. You walk like a man."

"It doesn't look like anybody lives here. And if nobody lives here, nobody will notice my thumb marks or my heavy feet!"

She pushed into the hallway, where a series of doors displayed themselves, ready to be perused by her. The first door unveiled a shabby bathroom—she turned the overhead light on and off quickly, unable to look at the dingy floors and spiderwebs on the ceiling. Next, she opened a closet, which had been emptied of all clothing and hangers.

"See!" Parker called out to Jake, waving her hand through the empty air. "Nothing. Nobody."

And then, she was standing in front of the final door. Greedily, she jerked the knob, but it didn't relinquish to her touch. Coming down from her high, Parker bit her lip bitterly and tried pulling it again, harder this time.

"It's locked," Jake annoyingly announced. He watched her struggle with his arms folded and an arrogant expression on his face.

"I understand," she shot back. She jostled and tugged it, fighting with the ancient lock until her arms burned.

"You've got to relax," Jake whispered. "I get it: You don't wanna think about what's waiting for us out there. But now you're seriously making too much noise, and you're gonna alert the wrong kinda person at this time of night."

"Don't talk down to me."

"I'm not. I'm just trying to prevent disaster. Either you're gonna attract attention, or you're gonna split the wood and ruin this little covert operation. Give it a rest, alright?"

Parker scowled at Jake but heeded his warning. Crouching down, she pulled a bobby pin out of her pocket—something she packed as a last resort. She always saw people using them on TV but wasn't convinced it was a legitimate way to pick a lock. She spread the fine wire and shoved one end of the pin into the keyhole. She rummaged it around, hoping she'd be able to feel the correct gears turning from within the rusty hardware.

"This is just stupid now," Jake grumbled.

It pissed Parker off that suddenly, he wanted to be suave and unaffected again. Why couldn't there just be one version of Jake? Why was he always changing himself, assuming a role he thought he was meant to occupy? Victim. Machismo. Indifferent artist. She questioned her attraction to him—maybe there was only one facade she liked, and that veneer wasn't authentic. It was just the personality he knew Parker wanted from him, and so he rolled it out whenever he desired her affection. At his core, he was self-serving. That was the real him.

In her silent rage, Parker had shifted around enough gears, and one finally popped. The knob loosened with a *click*. "No way," Parker breathed, temporarily forgetting her agitation.

"Whoa," Jake gasped in agreement.

In a windowless room, an old computer sat on the floor, its blue monitor illuminating the peculiar space. The walls were covered in wooden planks, and the carpet was old, grey, and stained. The ceilings were a white textured emblem of the past. Nothing else rested with the computer—not a picture frame, lamp, or desk to work at. The ancient machine extended far and wide, the fans ceaselessly whirring as they fought to keep the device cool in such an airless room. The keyboard was just as retro, with dust collecting between the letters, and a mouse that struggled to scroll was plugged into the machine.

Parker stepped forward, but once again, Jake held her back. "Shh," he commanded and held a finger to his lips. He craned his neck, looking into the recesses of the home, his ears perked up.

Parker wasn't enraptured by the sounds, though, and only waited a brief moment before trying to storm into the room again. Jake didn't want to risk even a whisper from escaping the confines of the house and alerting the approaching person, but he didn't know what else to do. Parker was doing as Parker always did: acting defiantly. Antsy, he continued to swivel his head, trying to reach the sound with his ear drums. He concentrated until the rustling of the garbage bags out back made themselves known again. He waved at her furiously—it was time to go.

She was about to touch the keyboard, ready to berate Jake for his unrelenting nervousness, when she heard it, too. Footsteps. Unmistakable footsteps lumbering toward the house from the back entrance.

"Shit," Parker snapped under her breath. "What do we do?"

"Leave. Like, right now," Jake quietly urged.

"From where?" Now Parker was beginning to panic—it was her facade that was crumbling. Theorizing about the situation was one thing, but to actually be in it was another. Her throat burned, the remnants of the last murderer's fingers still branded on her skin: an insidious reminder.

"Front door," Jake instructed.

He quickly dove into the room, grabbed her hand, and shut the door behind them. Scurrying across the floor on their toes, they checked to make sure the coast was clear—first glancing out the window, then making use of the peephole. Jake held his breath as he unlocked the ancient knob. The commotion was building out back. Parker's hands were clammy. All she could think about was Sheriff Heston. He was on her. Holding her down. Squeezing her vital bones, trying to break them.

"Just go!" she practically bellowed.

Stunned, Jake flung the door open, and out the two of them went. Parker made a break for the truck while Jake lingered at the entrance, gently latching the door without causing a scene. Parker was in the passenger seat, her vision growing blurry as tears threatened to spring down her cheeks.

"Please, hurry," she mumbled to herself. She rocked back and forth, her heart beating at an unnatural pace. She couldn't handle it. Parker didn't have the car keys. She couldn't take off. She couldn't leave. "Please."

Jake was finally beside her; the worry drained from his countenance now that he actually had a purpose: save Parker. The engine revved to life, and Jake peeled out of the parking space, careful not to hit the gas too hard lest he leave a mark. He only flicked the headlights on when they were back on the country highway, and Thorton had faded into the darkness. Nobody pursued them.

Chapter 7

"We should have stayed," Parker announced.

They were back at her place after a tense ride home. Parker had been reduced to tears, attempting to stifle her sobs while she kept her eyes trained out the window, hoping Jake couldn't see the wetness on her cheeks. But of course, he knew she was crying. Her sobs were guttural, even if muffled by taut fingers clamped over her mouth, and her whole body uncontrollably trembled. He offered comfort, reaching a handover and placing it on her lap. She brushed it off, though, not wanting to feel wounded.

But once they were parked in her driveway, Parker flipped a switch. The sanctuary that was her home enveloped her again, and her mind was no longer in a state of shock. Ideas began to swarm her, adrenaline replacing the anguish in her veins. She was brimming with excitement—potential—now. Jake was perplexed by her newfound ambition, following after her like the lost puppy he showed himself to be at the hacker's house. Parker scoffed as he struggled to keep up, dazed and begging for answers that she wasn't ready to divulge yet.

Perhaps she was overcorrecting, attempting to mask the humiliation that superseded her surprise outburst. But she didn't have time to ruminate on that. She didn't have time for anything other than the investigation. She just had to push through, knuckles white as she buried the thoughts that threatened to consume her.

"Maybe we could have caught him," she continued.

"You've lost your mind," Jake murmured.

"We gave up too easily."

"Parker, we're not superheroes—"

"Who said we're dealing with a jacked-up villain?"

She paced around the living room, and Jake followed her with his gaze. He sank into the couch, unenthused but making no attempts to leave. He was invested in the show that was Parker Rose, and for some reason, the attention burned her ass. The focus she craved came only to her at the wrong time for the wrong reasons. She winced whenever she regarded him, and his eyes were studying her every twitch.

"What are you looking for, Parker?"

"The hacker!" she replied, flabbergasted.

"Yes, but... alright," he motioned for her to stop, "calm down. Please."

"I'm calm. I'm also just—just *thinking*."

"You're worked up."

She was torn—his countenance was sincere, but she always managed to put her foot in her mouth whenever he coerced her into a mild-mannered discussion. He had ulterior motives. Maybe he was in the same boat as her, quietly regretting his prior behavior, and now he wanted the higher ground. He desired to be the protector, the voice of reason, and the saving grace to her inquest that was spiraling out of control. She sat beside him anyway, a sore pout on her lips. God, how she was reduced to a childlike state when she was with him.

"Let's start from the beginning," Jake offered. "Somebody has been hacking into the devices of doctors and demanding a ransom. That hack has been linked to a source located in Thorton. Though the house looks abandoned, someone still has regular access to it. We know this because of the amount of garbage and the fact that they showed up tonight."

"Without a vehicle, too."

"Really?"

"Yeah," Parker shrugged, "I mean, we definitely would have heard someone pull up to the house; there wasn't anything in the driveway, and none of the cars we saw earlier had been moved. We didn't hear this person walk around the side of the house, so they entered through the backyard."

"Unless they parked a block away."

Parker bit her lip. "That's possible."

"So, what do we do with all this?"

"Well, we have to consider this IP address is another fake. Think about it: The people who allegedly live in that home are just as untraceable as the hack itself. Maybe articles and online documents have been fucked with to hide the real identity of the person living there, and maybe not even for malicious reasons. Maybe the hacker knows whoever lives there isn't tech savvy and would never realize that somebody else has assumed the identity of their home address."

"Then, what about the computer?"

"The thing was ancient. Looked to be unused and forgotten about. Again, there's always the chance that the hacker has gained access to the only device in the house and is routing their location through it so that nobody can find the true source of these malware attacks. The real owner of that computer will be none the wiser and won't know how to help any investigators who do show up to take a look at it because they don't know how to operate the thing. They don't even have a desk for it."

"It's just... it sounds like our guy is making a lot of assumptions."

"And that could lead us to a fault in their plan. It can't all be airtight if they're puppeteering this from a distant location."

"I don't know. It seems so outlandish. The hacker goes to great lengths to... swindle a few small-town doctors?"

"If the hacker is smart—and it seems like they are—all of this can be done with a few keystrokes. Hell, maybe this isn't as impersonal as you've been saying it is. They've got a reason to go after Dr. Ang and Marshal, and so they've done everything within their power to make it an effective con."

"Nah..."

"Oh, for once in your fucking life, don't be so logical."

Jake smirked as if this was the trap he had been waiting for Parker to fall into. She silently cursed herself when she realized what she had done. "You agree, then? This is a wild conspiracy you've made up?"

"I didn't mean it like that. Don't twist my words."

"I'm not doing anything."

"Exactly! You're not doing anything. You're hounding me for details, to tag along, to know more about this elusive case, and yet when it comes time to actually try to figure it out, you just default to *random. Totally not targeted. All in your head, Parker.* I don't understand what's so crazy about two people in Watson Bay having done something bad that they actually need to pay for."

"There you go again, siding with the hacker," Jake barked. "I get that *you* are all impressed by this scheme because all you've ever known is small-town crime—petty theft, maybe some insurance fraud. But nobody ever finds themselves caught up in a big mystery. So now you're determined to blow things out of proportion just to satisfy your boredom."

"And that's different from what you're doing, how?"

Parker inched closer to Jake, hoping to break the stoicism he'd been sitting with. Agitate him into movement. Even better, maybe she could cross enough boundaries that he'd get out of her house. She was sick of this discussion, always trying to mince her words so that Jake wouldn't jump down her throat the moment she uttered a syllable he didn't like. The more he clung to her, the more painful these arguments became. Was she truly so terrible that he had made it his life's mission to berate her? Any normal person would have grown tired of the flogging by now. Yet Jake persisted, finding new ways to catch Parker off guard and wrangle her into a confession of immorality.

"I'm trying to be the voice—"

"Of reason," they proclaimed in unison.

"I knew it. I knew that's why you stayed," Parker groaned. "You lie and lie and lie, claiming to want to look out for me and actually, like, help me when it comes to this shit, and then you just rub my failures in my face."

"Well, tonight *was* a bust."

"No, it wasn't! We've seen the computer, and you know what? We should go back for it before the hacker wises up. And we know that somebody lives there. Even if they aren't our suspect, their obliviousness could still be a clue. Maybe the hacker's assumed identity isn't random, but the ransomware attacks are. I don't know. But we've got something!"

"Actually, you could've had this whole mess resolved by now if you just put half as much energy into breaking the code, not running around the county with me."

"You wanted to come!"

"Okay, and? Sure, I'm used to a little more adventure and chaos in my life. Maybe I am just using you for a small thrill, but I always wind up at home, alone and feeling empty because nothing we've done will ever compare to real danger. It will never make a real impact."

"What are you talking about? We were both in the midst of a murder plot last year."

"That already came and went. It's history now. We're back to living in a small, dumpy town with small-brained civilians who click on obvious phishing links and follow them to their logical end: ransomware. The other idiots who've been victimized by this pathetic scam are too ashamed to come ask you to deal with it. Or better yet? They've already heard through the grapevine that there's nothing you can do about it. You're just taking money and offering vague platitudes. Everyone's better off heading to the superstore and buying a new computer."

Parker saw red as Jake lamented against her, and for a brief moment, she wished she could break something. The TV, a window, his hand. How dare he come into her home and antagonize her. He thought of her the way he accused the hacker of thinking of her peers: guinea pigs to test their demented theories on. He was idling through life with her, waiting until he was finally ready to move back to New York, where intelligent people led interesting lives and discussed their grandiose careers. She was nothing more to him than a punching bag, and she was sick of accepting the blows, hoping that one day they'd find a common ground. That they'd become the couple she had fashioned in her brain. Her feelings had gotten the better of her, even if she had tried long and hard to beat them into submission, to remind them of the reality that was unfolding before her. Jake was a viciously duplicitous man.

"I'm speaking in generalizations," Jake clarified, watching the expression on Parker's face intensify.

"Don't lie," she retorted. "You literally just said I'm a lazy scammer myself."

"I didn't mean it like that."

"Then what did you mean, huh? What the fuck are you doing here if you hate me so much?"

"I don't hate you, Parker." His tone was earnest, and the sound of it dripping off his tongue made her nauseous. He really was good at playing this part—the part of the lovelorn fool who kept saying the wrong thing at the wrong time. What was Parker supposed to do with that? Forgive him?

"Bullshit. You've hated me since day one. I wouldn't immediately believe you, and you've nursed that grudge ever since."

"How come you didn't?"

"Because obvious answers are usually the correct ones. You've been ranting about that since I brought the ransomware attacks to you. The murders were on your property, all security footage was wiped, and you had mysteriously convinced everyone of your innocence. Major red flag, Jake, and you know it, so don't pretend like I was making leaps and bounds to arrive at that conclusion. That's just dishonest."

"Obvious doesn't always equate to easy, though. I was the easy suspect, not the obvious one."

Parker sighed and pinched the bridge of her nose as she fought back the tears that prickled against her skin. Why couldn't she get ahold of herself? "I get that you don't know what it's like to grow up feeling safe, to learn to trust everyone and everything around you, but it's difficult, okay? It's difficult to become an adult and have all that alleged shelter come crumbling down around you. Sheriff Heston wasn't just a cop; he was... he was someone I trusted to my very core. He'd been looking after this whole town my entire life. I had no reason to think it was him because I had decades of good behavior to corroborate that.

"That's why I haven't left Watson Bay. That's why I still have trouble imagining it. The outside world has more killing, more backstabbing, more insecurity than I will ever have here. Or at least that's what I used to think because I'm scared that this is a pattern. Sheriff Heston revealed something ugly about this place, and now I'm struggling to wrap my mind around it. And I don't wanna keep vouching for people just 'cause I grew up with them, and they treated me with decency when I was a kid. I could be covering for the next murderer, the next hacker... and for what? For loyalty?

"So I get it, Jake. I was wrong about you, but that doesn't mean I'm gonna keep being wrong about everything."

He clenched his jaw, the muscles moving under his flesh tersely. She had struck something, but by the darkness that clouded his eyes, she could tell it wasn't about to resonate with him. It wasn't going to bring peace between them. He pursed his lips, giving her that defeated smile one often flashed whenever they had given up on arguing because they deemed their opponent to be a lost cause.

"I think you're trying to shield yourself from any blame by taking a stance based on an inflated sense of morality," he uttered succinctly.

Parker slumped in her seat, unsure why she expected a different outcome. "And I think you should leave, Jake."

He was already getting up before she could finish her sentence. He didn't look at her, didn't mutter a halfhearted goodbye. Jake grabbed his jacket off the coat rack, waltzed out the door, and jumped in his car. He was gone before she could take a full five breaths, and Parker felt his absence in her bones this time. She should have been relieved to finally be rid of the man who treated her with so much disdain, and yet the hollowness of her false victory ached. Fighting never felt good, even when she knew that she was in the right. It left her wanting more, an insatiable thirst she feared would never be quenched without receiving Jake's unconditional love. Something she was certain she'd go her entire life without.

So, Parker had to keep moving. She had to fill her brain with ideas, lines of code, and questions to ask. She had to see the investigation through to the end, unrelenting in her pursuit until the hacker was revealed and harmony restored. Watson Bay wasn't going to be eroded by greed and violence—she couldn't lose something she loved to a few bored miscreants. Besides, there was something strange going on at that house, and Parker was certain it would unravel a host of clues. She would go back, but she would do it bravely this time. No tears, no whining, no pesky memories.

A phone buzzed in her pocket, breaking her monologue. She pulled it out, and was staring at a new message on Dr. Ang's cell:

Tick-tock. Tick-tock. I can't wait forever for my payback, Doctor. Consider the updated price interest. $25k is to be sent in Bitcoin to wallet address bc13lm2.

Parker had to get back to work.

Chapter 8

Parker's phone woke her up with its incessant shrill. At first, her heart thumped at the idea of Jake blowing up her text messages. He was begging for her forgiveness, alright, determined to rectify the destruction he had caused with his calloused and inaccurate words. She ignored them for as long as she could muster, one ear surveilling the room as the *pings* and whistles continued their symphony. The sun hadn't even risen yet, which meant her precious sleep was being disrupted. Jake really couldn't let her alone.

However, when she finally tasked herself with rifling through the apologia, she was met with something far better than Jake groveling. She had a host of random numbers asking for her assistance:

I've been hacked!

My computer is locked. Please help :(

Parker—when do you open? I need phone ASAP. Typing from daughter's computer. She is upset with me for opening emails. Parents can't do anything right.

Her door was hot with desperate knuckles by the time she shuffled down the stairs. It was hours before her regular start to the day, but there was a lineup on her driveway. Her clients all wore scrubs and had worried looks fixed on their faces. They noticed her before she could scurry back up the stairs to put on something more becoming—she didn't want to greet her anxious customers with tattered slippers and a fuzzy pink robe. But they were calling out to her, beckoning her to unlock the door and let them in. Hear them out. With a defeated sigh, Parker opened the floodgates.

"I don't know what happened," claimed one woman Parker had only ever encountered at the grocery store. Her blue attire was decorated with colorful patches—she likely worked with sick children. "I was just online shopping, nothing out of the ordinary. I been on that site so many times before, too, but maybe I typed something wrong into the search bar, and I was brought to a similar store. Either way, my card was charged, and ten minutes later, I had an alert on my phone that I now owed twenty-five *grand*. Parker, I don't got that kind of money."

"And you won't be forced to pay it," Parker assured her and accepted the cell.

"I haven't even used my laptop in months," professed a young man. "I've been at the hospital so much I don't have time for watching TV or writing something—I don't know—at home. Maybe the virus latched onto me when I connected my phone to a public Wi-Fi network, but my phone is fine. For now." His resolve broke. "I'm usually so good about these things... I just don't understand how it happened."

"Are you being asked for a ransom?"

"Yep," he sheepishly confessed.

"Then, I don't think you can blame yourself for this one."

"Is this... are we being targeted?" he asked in a hushed tone.

Parker gave a meek nod, trying not to attract attention. "That's my theory, anyway."

Every brand new patron had a similar story: They don't know how or why they brought this upon themselves; they usually remained wary of scams, didn't answer the phone for unknown numbers, and never checked their junk folders, yet they were still attacked. Parker jotted down each individual tale, taping the note to the confiscated device, and piled them on every available surface. She assured her clientele they had nothing to be worried about—every lost document was recoverable, and if they were being honest with her, then there was nothing so invaluable or incriminating that they couldn't be without it for the next couple of weeks. At the end of the torrent of confused customers, Parker had about 30 computers and phones at her disposal, all of them blockaded by the same ransom request. She had struck gold.

Elatedly, she made herself a massive breakfast and gorged on her feast of eggs, toast, and coffee while she waded through the materials, sorting them by the infecting scam. Phishers went in one bucket, innocuous website visitors in another, and the ones with a source that had yet to be revealed would be her first foray into the hacker's latest slate of attacks.

Her phone rang again. This time, she was excited to answer it. Either Jake would be miffed to hear her smug tale of malware treasure, or someone had another clue to offer her.

"Parker Rose?" a woman whimpered on the other line.

"This is she," Parker responded with satisfaction.

"I... I'm sorry to bother you."

"Not at all."

"I'm such an oaf, but... I... I'm in some real trouble." The lady on the other end cleared her throat. "We all are."

"What do you mean?"

"Can you please come to the hospital?"

***

What was normally a wasteland of bored nurses and hypochondriacal elderly was now hell on earth. Workers were manically plugging and unplugging vital machines into various outlets, files had been opened and torn through carelessly, and doctors were desperately investigating their malfunctioning phones, reporting their findings to each other with alarm. The once pleasant waiting room was a horror show of sickly patients waiting their turn, bundled up under layers of clothes and staring longingly at Parker.

"What's going on?" Parker asked while she strolled up to the desk.

The receptionist had already been crying. Black mascara was caked on her lashes, fused together by the wetness of her tears. Streaks of pink were revealed under her tainted foundation, and her scrubs were stained with multicolored splotches. The receptionist shook her frazzled head, ashamed to be confessing this to anyone, much less Parker, who had no authority or esteem. Parker could see it written on the woman's face: She was too old to have made such a mistake, and now some young girl was here to clean up the mess. It was humiliating.

"It's all gone," the receptionist wheezed. Parker patiently waited for her to explain, watching as her chest struggled with the rapid rise and falls of her ragged breathing. "I was stupid, I know that. I took over the desk early this morning, and maybe I was too tired—didn't have enough coffee, or whatever—but I checked my emails. I was bored, scrolling and clicking, and I... I saw something interesting come up. You know... I had recently entered the lottery, and I got this message saying there was a big surprise waiting for me. I thought, oh, they must've drawn the numbers. Sure enough, the email claimed to be awarding me a prize—a big one, too. I screeched and celebrated, called the hubby and told him the good news, but he said, 'Maxine, there ain't no lotto goin' on. Ain't nobody draw your ticket.' So I checked the news, and I'll be damned: nothing about any winners. That's when the... the message appeared."

"Twenty-five grand in ransom?" Parker asked knowingly.

"No," she replied tearfully. "I wish. That'd be too easy for us to pay off. Stuff happens like that all the time. I mean, not to a hospital as humble as ours, but we've been trained on it. Which is why I should've known better..."

"How much?"

Maxine drew in a deep inhale. "Ten million."

So much for Jake's theory about small potatoes, Parker thought bitterly.

"Can I take a look?" she inquired kindly.

"Sure thing." Maxine, still sitting in her chair, rolled out of the way, and Parker took her place at the monitor.

It really was all gone. People's entire histories had been erased from existence. There were no birth certificates, no medical records, no contact sheets. The backup drives that were designed for such a conundrum had been wiped clean, too. The paper trails only went so far back—Parker didn't need a staff member to report the obvious: Anyone born during the last couple of decades was in the computer, not in the basement neatly tucked into a filing cabinet. Even then, people who were currently in need couldn't always get what they were looking for—machines that were reliant on the computer system were useless. There wasn't another network for them to connect to or replacements that could override the issue. The hospital was completely offline. Except, miraculously, for the TV that continued to play.

"A devastating windstorm is predicted to hit Watson Bay county," a reporter announced like a harbinger of death. "It is currently pushing across the Pacific, building speed as pressure mounts. The windstorm is currently on track to hit these rural communities next week, and residents are being urged to collect provisions, look for appropriate shelter, and buckle up for a terrible ride."

"Do you think it's a coincidence?" Maxine asked softly.

"The storm?" Parker frowned. "I don't think the hacker could have predicted it."

"Yeah, but, don't you think it's a bit convenient? Windstorms may not harm the likes of you or me, but we get 'em regularly during the winter, and each time, old folks are coming in with all sorts of injuries. When you add the cold to that, the illnesses going around... We're at our most vulnerable right now."

"And you're not just being ransacked for money, but are being cut off from the world."

"Exactly. It's a conspiracy—"

Parker winced. "I wouldn't go that far."

"But you called them *the hacker*. You know who they are. We aren't the only people affected. Just today, most everyone came in complaining about a computer virus."

Parker fought the urge to ask Maxine why she still clicked on the link when she knew there was a widespread attack going on. It wouldn't be helpful to admonish the only person willing to verbally spar with her, bouncing ideas around until something finally fell into place. But it was painfully moronic, something Parker only thought intentionally stupid characters on television shows could accomplish. To think, if Jake were here, he'd berate Parker for even tepidly suggesting that perhaps Maxine was in on it despite such obvious tells.

"There will be power outages, too," Parker continued, reorienting her brain on the current task. "If this windstorm is anything like the one we had last year, even without the ransomware holding your guys hostage, you'd be swamped with problems." Parker paused. "Don't you guys have backup machines and generators for exactly this kind of thing? Shouldn't you be able to use them *now*?"

Maxine shook her head. "Sometimes, technology ain't always a good thing. Everything is hooked up to the internal network. And I mean *everything*."

"Is there anyone else I can talk to? Like a tech team you guys regularly call whenever you have computer problems?"

"You're the only person in this whole damned town, Parker. We ain't never had a reason to hire you before, is all."

"Well, shit," Parker muttered.

***

The house looked lonely. Despite their previous excursion's unfortunate end, Parker had no choice but to muster up the courage and drive herself back to the crime scene. The same trucks they had witnessed the first time around remained in their parking places, randomly lining the cracked asphalt. She had circled the block, evaluating the rear of the property in hopes of gaining an understanding of every potential entry point, of every potential variable. But there was no indication that the hacker was able to traverse multiple lawns in order to stalk through their own backyard, and no cars were present along the other side of the neighborhood. It appeared to Parker that she was alone. Hopefully, it would stay that way long enough for her to make a breakthrough.

With a deep breath, she opened the car door, pushing out into the night air and allowing it to swallow her for a moment like she needed to acclimate. The quiet was more oppressive without the accompaniment of Jake's shallow inhalations. Even her own lungs couldn't pierce the silence, creating a disembodied feeling as she took in air without being able to hear it.

The soles of her shoes faintly tapped against the concrete, and Parker flexed her fingers while she prepared to enter the house once more. Ducking around the side of the building, she didn't bother to check the windows. She just had to believe that it would all work out—the hacker would be gone for the evening, if they had ever been here at all, the doors would remain unlocked, and Parker would finally gain access to a crucial piece of information. She couldn't afford to think otherwise.

Strutting to the backdoor like she owned the place, Parker whipped it open. Thankfully, it yielded to her touch, and the inside of the abode was immediately accessible to her. No pain. No struggle. The interior still seemed abandoned, with all of the garbage just as they left it, the furniture dusty and unwrinkled by heavy bodies weighing it down. Her eyes didn't land upon stains marking up the floors, nor could she detect traces of her and Jake's foray into the house. With her nerves a little settled, she darted toward the computer room. The real test would be whether or not it had been disturbed.

Upon entering the hallway, claustrophobia began to push down on her shoulders. Her view of the house was blockaded by the tight walls, her movement was restricted to a sprint in only one direction, and noises were muffled by the densely packed plaster. Without Jake to stand guard, entering the sealed room was a risk. She gulped—she knew that when she came here. And if she didn't suck it up, a lot more people would be in danger. But she didn't remember this closed-off sect of the house feeling so daunting. She didn't remember the perspiration bubbling on her brow and trickling down her frigid skin. She didn't remember being so scared. Not until Jake told her to worry. Not until she had to run.

She turned the knob, bracing herself for the worst, but it unlatched. The room was empty, though she scrambled to dig her phone out of her pocket, shining the flashlight into the abyss to make sure her eyes weren't deceiving her. That she hadn't walked straight into a trap. She held her breath as the white light beamed into the void, illuminating the crevices that had previously been unknowable to her. She stood on her heels, braced to make a sudden movement should she come face-to-face with a monster. But no such creature arrived out of the darkness.

"You're alone, Parker," she muttered to herself. "Stop being such a pussy."

The computer screen, which continued to blaze blue, called out to her like a lighthouse in the midst of a storm. She dashed forward, crashing to her knees before the device, her fingerprints pulsating with desire. She began furiously tapping keys until the screen shifted, displaying a typical assortment of inconspicuous folders, widgets, and information about the make and model of the computer. It was nothing thrilling.

She opened files at light speed, poring through their contents in search of compelling words, fragments, or breadcrumbs. Parker didn't detect sequences that elicited suspicion or capabilities that aligned with the hacks themselves. All of the programs, including the internet, were outdated. The entire thing ran on software from the '90s, and the functionality of trying to perform such widespread and complex attacks appeared hopelessly slow. When attempting her own version of a hack, she was unable to retrieve evidence that such a feat had taken place utilizing the device before.

Furrowing her brow, she searched high and low through the computer's hard drive, following endless tunnels of files and folders that never seemed to populate anything more than another empty folder. Until she happened upon the end of the rainbow. A folder entitled *333* had actual data harvested within its pixelated environment. When Parker clicked on it, she gasped: Everyone's stolen information began to load. Names, addresses, credit card numbers, and bank accounts all sprang to life. They weren't sorted systematically—in fact, the downpour of data was overwhelming and troublesome to sift through. Parker wondered if her usual keyboard strokes would whip them into shape, but then again, actually reading the pilfered personal information didn't align with the hacker's motives.

Recalling what Dr. Ang said—the hacker already had access to her money, so why not take what they wanted?—Parker stopped trying to make sense of the array of victims. Proof of the hacker's accomplishments was just sitting on a computer, waiting to be pillaged by the first detective who bothered to look deeply into the matter. She didn't need a special cheat to populate the bounty of the hacker's heist; she merely succeeded through a maze of documents, nor could she discern anything legible about the hacker's motivation from the haul. It was just a juicy hunk of meat, specifically designed to be devoured without much thought. A diversion.

Bells seemed to go off in her head. The whole computer was a diversion. The peculiar locale, the ease with which she found herself scouring the contents of the device, and the type of information the computer received were all too convenient. This wasn't the main source of the virus—no, it was a jumping-off point. It sent out the commands and harvested the data but didn't construct the source code. It didn't produce the malware but simply beamed it out to the given targets.

She wondered if the device was being monitored religiously. If she moved it in order to better wait for the next command, would the hacker know? With every letter she punched into the machine, was the hacker watching to see which control she'd devise? The criminal was obviously two steps ahead of her, ahead of everyone, and knew this dupe would attract attention eventually.

It *was* a trap, albeit a useful one, for Parker could still ascertain information from the computer without arousing awareness from the hacker. She'd just have to gather more intel and devise a timeline for the next alleged attack. Then, she'd come back to the computer and camp out until the commands started to write themselves onto the machine. With that, she'd know what the hacker was doing exactly in order to infect the entire town of Watson Bay. Better yet, she'd probably be able to intercept it. She just had to be quick and alert and, importantly, keep the hacker oblivious to her scheme.

Gathering her things, Parker exited out of all the tabs she had opened. She lingered by the device until the computer's screen no longer reflected her interference, and it was just a blue light shining into the void. As she got up to retreat, she noticed one final piece of the puzzle. Something she felt stupid for having missed before. The computer was linked to the Watson Bay library network.

Chapter 9

The matted gray carpets smelled as though they hadn't been cleaned in centuries. Flies lethargically buzzed through the stale air, unafraid of getting caught. None of the patrons bothered to rid the quiet space of nuisances, especially not the staff, who sat behind plastic shields like they were receptionists at a prison. Parker felt like a scorned lover looking to visit her inmate boyfriend—judged, silly, and disconcerted by such a rank environment. The shelves were hardly stocked with material, leading Parker to wonder if anyone was making use of the library, and perhaps their lack of interest in reading was another score Jake was counting against them.

She rolled her eyes, the phantom whispers of Jake's arrogance dancing along the back of her neck. She bet he had been here on occasion, hoping to stumble across the literature he had grown accustomed to. The kind of material he expected as his God-given right. If he loved the intellectualism of New York so much, he should have stayed there. Parker caught herself gritting her teeth only when her jaw began to ache. She was having imaginary fights with a man who hadn't reached out in days. It was a waste of her time to fret over Jake's supposed beliefs anymore. If he had moved on, then so would she.

Stepping further into the sad atmosphere, Parker peeked into the computer room, lazily sectioned off by half a barren white wall, and took stock of her tools: twenty desktops, zero other computer users. She had the place to herself for now. Quietly celebrating, she turned her attention to the librarian—a stout lady with her wispy hair tucked into a crocheted beanie; two pairs of glasses, one around her neck and the other pressed close to her large eyes; and multiple sweaters hiding her small figure. She smiled warmly at Parker, which she took as a good sign, and marched over to the bleak desk.

"Hello," Parker paused to read her name tag, "Margaret."

"Well, hello—"

"Ms. Rose."

"Ah, yes, Ms. Rose." She attempted to mask her confusion in order to maintain her politeness. "Have I seen you before?"

"Oh, no," Parker admitted. "I actually have some questions for you."

"Alright—ask away."

"What does it take to get on one of those computers?" Parker pointed to the series of desks as if the librarian would have no clue what she was referring to.

"A library card, for starters."

Parker pulled out her wallet, sorting through the pile of useless plastic she carried with her everywhere. She had expired gift certificates to stores she'd never heard of, old credit cards that had been replaced twice over, and membership points to at least five fast-food restaurants. She did not, however, possess a library card.

"I guess we'll need to sign me up today," Parker announced. She handed Margaret her ID and attempted to observe the computer screen through the librarian's lenses. "But are there other rules for using the computers?" she continued.

Margaret sighed. "Please refrain from doing anything... *inappropriate* on public devices."

Parker immediately blushed. "Fuck, jeez, ah... no, I just meant like time limits. Are there time limits? I have a paper to write, is all, and my computer's down, so I'll need to be here all day pretty much," she fibbed.

The librarian eyed her for a moment but accepted the story without any pushback. "You'll get a unique code which'll allow you one hour of usage. Normally, we'd cap you at that, but furthering your studies is always a good excuse to hog up resources."

"So, the computers are pretty popular?"

"Maybe. I don't know. People aren't usually fighting over them if that's what you mean."

"Then why the time limits?"

Margaret gave Parker a look. "Inappropriate usage."

Parker flushed red once again. "Gotcha." She thought for a second, and then, "Is there a database of all the computer users? And what they're looking at? In case of, you know, crime?"

"That is confidential information, Ms. Rose." Margaret's tone was inscrutable.

"I'm just assuming that by the sound of it, this kinda stuff happens often, and it would be useful to be able to catch the pervs—I mean perps."

"The library handles it." Margaret slid a brand new library card across the desktop, along with a little slip of paper for Parker to use as her login. "Come back in an hour," she instructed.

Parker accepted the offering and scurried to a computer cut off from the rest of the world. She couldn't have the screen visible to anyone, especially if she wanted to keep her ruse going. She had perhaps asked too many questions and made herself dubious in the eyes of the librarian. Excited to start her work, though, Parker hurriedly typed in the automated username, sinking into her seat as if to hide her glee. But her high didn't last. Like all things in Parker's life, her successes were always a slippery slope right back down to the bottom.

Each button she pressed took about a minute to populate on the screen. Whenever she made an error, she had to wait another 60 seconds for the computer to finally catch on. She hoped it was merely a fluke, that once she was inside the system, things would run a lot smoother, but she should have known that the underfunded and underused machines would pose a problem. Equally as outmoded as the command and control computer, Parker was flummoxed as to how the hacker was making use of such shoddy devices. Perhaps this was another dead end, and Parker was failing to recognize such obvious machinations of this game of cat and mouse. Then again, what better way to throw off your opponents than by harnessing seemingly obsolete computers?

By the time Parker had surpassed the login page, she was already frustrated. Biting the inside of her cheek, she punched in the commands to access the administrative features. Unsurprisingly, several minutes lapsed between each number she typed. She considered switching machines, wondering if she had picked the faulty one. Jumping to the seat beside her, she was able to type quicker and have the screen reflect her impressions, but the login failed—it was already in use. With her head swung low, she retreated to the librarian's desk in search of help.

"I need another username," Parker decried.

"Oh?" replied Margaret.

"Yeah. That computer doesn't work. I have to get on a different one."

"I'm not sure you'll have better luck."

"I don't have time to waste, though." Parker almost snapped but adjusted her tone, "My paper is due at midnight, and I haven't even started. I'm just... stressed."

Margaret was already printing another pass for Parker. "The next computer better be the only computer," she warned.

"I thought you said I could come back every hour?"

"Yes, but... I don't wanna see you hopping around. Do your work, stay in one place, and don't do anything inappropriate—"

Parker ripped the login ticket from Margaret's hand. "Got it, got it."

Arriving back at her station, the first computer she'd chosen was still struggling to load the user database. With a gruff sigh, Parker restarted the process on the computer beside it, enjoying the faster speed with which it worked, but worried that when she inevitably faced another roadblock, she wouldn't be able to do much about it. She was a hacker, sure, but she wasn't a miracle worker. She couldn't revive sluggish software and stilted screens. Especially not when there were over a dozen devices at her disposal, and any number of them could have been disseminating the ransomware attacks. If she were lucky, it wouldn't matter which specific computer the hacker had used so long as she could access the code they had planted. But the hacker wouldn't make it that easy. Parker feared she'd be coming back on a daily basis, playing musical chairs until she unlocked the correct computer.

Once inside the database, she was temporarily stalled by an encryption. Parker was rather impressed by the multitude of steps and barriers she faced, and while she easily evaded the cipher, she wondered if perhaps the other institutions in town should take a page out of the library's book. At the very least, the lady at the front desk of the hospital needed to have a chat with Margaret about internet safety.

While the list slowly trickled onto the page one name at a time, Parker plugged the identities into her phone, hoping to double the rate by which she could investigate every individual. However, most names belonged to citizens she knew, and the others she needn't bother to Google—they were obviously fake. *Bill Williams. Seymour Buds.* Juvenile epithets the hacker subsumed like a taunt. Not only were they eons ahead of Parker, but they were bold enough to rub it in her face.

The obviousness of the pseudonyms made Parker retract her earlier sentiments about Margaret's alleged superiority. She must have been the one filling out the forms and fashioning IDs for the hacker—could she not recognize the sarcasm in their varying names? Did she not clock that the same person was trying to receive numerous library cards? Unless the hacker had found a way to authenticate their own usernames, effectively surpassing the need for Margaret's intervention entirely.

"Does it even matter?" Parker muttered to herself.

Every receptionist in town could have been in on the heist, but it wouldn't aid Parker in cracking the malware. Any accusation she made would be scoffed at, for the connection between desk jockeys and Bitcoin ransoms wasn't immediately obvious, and all Parker could offer up as proof was the sheer ignorance of the women supposedly safeguarding some old computer systems. This time, she wouldn't be lamenting about the new kid in town, either. She'd be trying to raise the alarm on elderly ladies who spent the majority of their days with their heads down and their lips sealed. She'd be shunned for attempting to make more Sheriff Heston's out of the innocent. Just as Jake said. She hated that she couldn't stop doubting her instincts. She didn't know what threads to follow anymore.

Aimless, Parker opted to decode the entire computer system, hoping through pattern recognition and the process of elimination that she'd find the strands of ransomware the hacker had buried. She'd been complaining about the state of the devices, but she grew up fiddling around with similar technology. She had dusty desktops stacked in her home, some of them remnants of her father's excursions in hacking. He was the one who taught her how to break into a mainframe, write her own commands, and trace other devices. He had helped her develop her technological prowess on worse-off machines, and yet Parker couldn't access that knowledge anymore. She couldn't be the astute little girl with an eye for the important details, patient and diligent enough to solve any cipher put before her.

Maybe it would have been different if her dad were still around. Sometimes, she acted as though he had died just because her parents had decided to move elsewhere, and she forgot she could give him a call. But they were the ones who told her to leave Watson Bay, who warned her to stop clinging to a nothing town filled with nothing people. She was better than that, and part of her wanted to defy them. To prove that Watson Bay was worth building a new life in. She could hear them on the other end, though—*stop fucking around and go make something of your life*. They wouldn't be impressed by her tales of private investigation and small-town syndicates. They would roll their eyes and remind Parker that they weren't interested in anything that didn't push the plot forward.

It didn't always used to be like that. There was a time in her life when Parker could rely on her father for just about anything. Had she been 12 and brought her discoveries to him, he would have helped her in a heartbeat. Was she really that emotionally stunted that she was being treated as a failure for the sake of tough love? Or had youth clouded her judgment, feigning a reality in which her parents loved her? She needed to believe that in order to thrive, but adulthood called all of her preconceived notions into question. Unless she truly was the problem, which everyone had been trying to tell her. Her lifestyle, her career, her personality—it had all melded into something unlikeable. That was why she was alone.

Her eyes burned as she stared at the screen, and yet nothing was making sense. She couldn't punch the right keys or read the strands of code. She was as useless as the machine, whirring and humming, overheating and cracking, incapable of performing as designed. Why was she here anymore?

She got up from the desk and retrieved another computer pass, hoping a quick stroll around the building would ignite something within her. She spent another hour blankly staring at the screen. Repeating this a few more times, Parker strove to believe that she could will herself into action. That she could conjure the person everyone expected her to be and what she had yet to become to spring from her chest like a burst pipe.

"Closing time," Margaret announced as she started the process of turning off all the lights.

Parker was almost relieved to be dismissed, like packing up, giving in, wasn't her idea. But she knew she couldn't keep lying like this to herself and everyone. She was flailing hard, and there would be dire consequences.

"Did you finish your essay?" the librarian asked on the way out.

Parker shrugged defeatedly.

"Ah, so I'll be seeing you again."

"Maybe." Parker wanted to sprint to her car. "Maybe not."

Chapter 10

Parker was holed up at the hacker's house. She found herself driving there after her botched attempt at mining the library computers for answers, and continued to return on a nightly basis, compelled by the machine and its mysterious glow. Nobody came around anymore. Perhaps the first night it happened was a fluke, or maybe the hacker had caught on to her routine and was letting her drive herself crazy staring at the computer. Nevertheless, Parker resolved that she wasn't smart enough to run any encryptions, so she may as well resort to the easiest course of action: sitting and waiting for the next virus to explode.

It was also the perfect cover for her inability to answer the phone. Her clients were growing impatient, the hospital remained out of commission with all other attempts at recovery failing, and Parker still didn't have anything to provide. No updates, breakthroughs, or consolations. She informed anyone who hounded her that she was working diligently and that she'd be off the grid while she conducted her investigation in an effort to keep her findings away from the hacker. But really, she just couldn't face the people she was currently letting down. She couldn't hear another story about someone's elderly father driving hours into the next county for healthcare, clutching his aching chest as the heart murmurs intensified. The guilt trips were smothering her, eking the last dregs of air from her lungs and brain until she melted to the floor and never woke up. That would have been preferable to her current fate, actually.

The hacker's house wasn't cozy. Noises kept her alert, her legs pressed to her chest while she rocked back and forth. The blue light was ingrained in her retinas, tainting the house with a sordid hue whenever she broke her gaze. She feared she'd be blind by the time the hacker did decide to make their presence known and wouldn't be able to fend them off with her self-inflicted impairment. She brought canned goods and bags of chips to eat, but nothing sustained her energy. Parker was withering away on the mildewy carpet, more lost in her mission than ever before.

The longer she stayed, the likelier it was she'd get caught. Even if it wasn't by the hacker, her car being parked on the side of a nearly abandoned road was sure to rouse suspicion from the straggling locals. It wasn't like squatting was permitted just because Parker was certain she'd caught her suspect, but at the very least, she hadn't broken anything and wasn't trying to steal the homeowner's belongings, either. Getting dragged out by the cops would certainly be humiliating, but it strangely wasn't the worst thing that could happen to her.

Parker was in a daze, losing track of time except for the gnawing dread that told her she was losing. Losing everything. What if the hacker wasn't going to strike again? The hospital was the big finale, and Parker was chasing a source that would never crop up on her radar. Maybe they'd even received part of their ransom and felt the loot was enough to disappear with. She thought she was doing something, however minimal, by attempting to guess the hacker's next move, but in the grand scheme of terrorizing the healthcare system, there wasn't anywhere to go after the hospital. And she should have realized that days ago.

Darkness swelled, notifying Parker of the Earth's rotation around the sun once again. At some point, she'd have to face Watson Bay. That moment was edging even closer, especially as the computer screen continued to emanate its single blank color. Unchanging. She gazed at it anyway, beginning to draw comfort from the unnatural hue. It lulled her to sleep, and she relented to her desires. Her exhaustion. She couldn't do anything about the hacker, the malware, anymore—she simply had to let go.

***

Parker's phone was alight. At first, she thought she had been mentally transported back a week. The day the hospital was cut off. It felt like a nightmare now, the relentless ringing of her phone as the desperate pleas for help enveloped her. She had to make it stop. She couldn't be haunted anymore.

Opening her eyes, she snatched her cell, ready to throw it against the wall. But then, through the dim glow of the early morning hours, she saw that her phone wasn't generating hallucinations. *WATSON BAY POLICE DEPT* blazed across the screen. She ignored it, unlocking her device and checking her missed calls. For the last hour, the police station had been ringing her every 30 seconds. Text messages assaulted her device, one after the other, demanding she pick up the phone. Could it be?

She looked at the computer, which seemed to carry a new aura. It was warmer than usual—freshly commanded. Parker checked the interface for any evidence of the hack, her frustration mounting as she realized what she had done. How could she have missed the latest hack? She had been here for centuries, biding her time until something happened, something she could trace. And now that that moment was here, she had squandered it once more, opting to give in to her selfish whims rather than do her fucking job.

Her phone rang again. "I'll be there!" she shouted into the receiver.

"Damn, Rose," the officer muttered on the other end.

"Sorry," she corrected hoarsely. "I'll be there."

***

Parker sat in the parking lot for a moment, staring at her haggard reflection in the rearview mirror. She furiously combed through her matted hair, attempting to look presentable, and doused her fingers in bottled water, which she rubbed along her tired eyes. She wore a puffer jacket, a smelly sweatshirt, and a pair of jeans she had stowed in the trunk after purchasing them some months ago. She looked neither professional nor reliable, something Jake had often scolded her for, but she wasn't about to let another opportunity slip through her fingers by dashing home to spruce up her appearance. She was going to suffer through the morning in order to gather crucial intel. This was what she needed to finally prop herself back up.

The sun had nearly crested the horizon, but the dull, overcast skies drowned it out, rendering the landscape shrouded in shadows. Parker readied her pen and notebook while she walked, hoping her preparedness would override her freakish phone call and unsightly appearance. When she walked into the police station, though, she realized her outfit would be the last thing on anyone's mind.

Officers rushed between desks with their heads bowed, ashamed to look Parker in the eye as she evaluated the scene. The receptionists had abandoned their posts, and incarcerated individuals howled with glee as the police struggled to book them. Parker was immediately taken by the arm and rushed into an interrogation room.

With the door shut tightly behind them, the officer grabbed her jacket and bag, placed them messily on the desk, and faced her with his arms resting on his hips. "Do you know what the fuck is happening?" he asked curtly.

"Nice to see you, too, Paul," Parker chided.

"Well, I was kind of hoping I'd never have to see you again."

"Wow, I really leave a good impression," Parker attempted to joke, but her cadence didn't convey the airy attitude she was aiming for.

"No, not like that," Paul insisted. "I meant... I was hoping I could solve this stuff from now on. You know, become sheriff?"

Parker stifled a laugh. Paul was a well-meaning guy, but he certainly wasn't the big brains of the Watson Bay department. He was still young, in his late twenties, and had a boyish look to him. His blond hair was cropped, his blue eyes piercing, but his cheeks were full of childish fat that he sought to cover up with a permanent scowl affixed to his weak brows. He would be well into his fifties before he started to develop the mannish features he desired, and even then, that wouldn't improve his lack of investigative instincts. Still, he was always willing to throw himself headfirst into a project, and Parker admired that.

"Oh, right..." Parker replied coolly. "So, you guys have been hacked?"

He nodded his head. "Yeah."

"When did it happen?"

"Sometime this morning. I'm thinkin' one. I didn't hear about it until I came in around four, though. Nobody's really fessing up."

"What do you mean?"

"It's obvious someone had to let the virus in," Paul revealed. "We were called in to look at the hospital after they got hijacked, and sure enough, we got hit with the same thing. Except the receptionist lady admitted to opening up a scam email, and none of our crew will admit to a damn thing. We're just supposed to believe it was an accident." He rolled his eyes and curled his fingers between his belt loops.

"You think you guys have another traitor in your midst?" Parked inched toward him, aglow with intrigue as the receptionist-led coop she'd been dreaming of may have come to fruition.

"No," he gasped. "Nothin' like that. We've been real good about profiling and all that since Heston. We just have too many proud folks walkin' these halls. Don't seem like Watson Bay is worth more to them than their pride."

"Figures," Parker grumbled, deflated once more. "Well, I think finding the *who* is less crucial than finding our actual offender—the hacker."

"You got any leads on that? The hospital wouldn't tell me much except that you were handling it."

"I found the IP address, but I haven't actually caught anyone stationed there sending out malicious attacks. Unless you count the command and control computer as the actual perp. Or, I guess, an unwitting accomplice."

Paul pursed his lips, studying Parker between squinted eyes as he parsed through her language. He didn't understand a word.

"So," she continued, "every device has an address, kinda like a house. Whenever you log onto the internet, your computer's location is tracked so things can be sent to it. These are rarely static, especially if you use your computer in a bunch of places. Our guy seems to be sending out these viruses from a sole machine that I located by finding the legit address connected to the network. Which I then went to and have spent many days there. The home is pretty much abandoned, but I did manage to find the source of all our problems."

"Alright, cool," Paul nodded lamely. "So, let's go destroy it."

"What?"

"Smash it to pieces," he shrugged. "I don't know. Unplug it and then cut up all its wires."

Parker giggled. "Okay, maybe that would help us in the short term and confuse the hacker for a couple hours, but that's not going to solve anything."

"But our guy won't have his virus maker anymore."

"Yes, he will because this computer I found is only delivering messages and signals. It's being told what to do by another system, which may or may not be a device at the library."

"Okay, we'll go and smash those up, too."

"If that's your only solution to this problem, then you're gonna have to go to the power plant and smash all that shit up, too. Then, the cell phone towers, and the internet companies, and every satellite that can access Watson Bay. We'd all have to go completely off the grid."

"It won't get that bad before the hacker finally gives up. He can go ask somebody else for millions of dollars."

"I don't think it's about the money," Parker replied while shaking her head. "What threat did you guys receive, anyway?"

"Oh, corruption and cover-ups, we'll pay for our crimes, hand over ten million in bitcoin... that kinda stuff."

"Was anyone named?"

"No, but we have to assume they're talking about Heston. He's the only skeleton we got in our closet."

"That can't be true."

"It sure is!" Paul crossed his arms defiantly and stood taller, meaning to impress Parker with his bodily assuredness.

"Really? No injustice, false accusations, and entanglement with criminals in the entire time that Watson Bay has been a town? Which is what—a couple hundred years?"

He sucked his lips. "Alright, well, maybe not that long. But I've been here for a couple years, and I haven't seen anything funny." Parker gave him a look, and he crumbled. "I dunno..."

"Well, the hacker definitely has a personal vendetta, and I doubt they'll stop until whatever it is they're after is settled. Done away with."

"Which is not the money?"

"Doubtful." She observed the disquieting space in which a large tinted window stared at them ominously. "What kind of firewall are you guys using, anyway?" she asked after a while.

"Normal stuff," Paul said. "Ad blockers, the anti-virus software that came with the computers, and something else I'm not too sure of. The fire department set us up with it."

"Must not be any good if a simple phishing scam can break through it," Parker replied. "Hell, I've hacked this place a couple times. I'm certain I could install some malware undetected, too."

"Hey," Paul whined, "you can't be doing that."

"Ugh, come on, Paul. I did it for research."

"What'd you find?"

"Nothing I can tell you."

Paul shook his head but decided to back off. They had more important matters to tend to. "When do you think this hacker will strike again?"

"Honestly, I'm not sure. I was starting to give up on tracing their attacks. I'd been waiting by that damn command and control computer for days when you called."

"You didn't see anything?"

"I was... I was asleep," Parker admitted shamefully. She leaned against the desk, her eyes trained on her muddy shoes scuffing up the concrete floors. Paul didn't reprimand Parker, but he didn't respond either, so she kept on, "I know we have that big storm coming. If anything, the hacker will use that to their advantage. They may or may not take down more infrastructure before then, though. Only time will tell."

"And our systems? Can you get 'em back up? Even if it's not perfect—"

"Not until I catch the hacker, Paul. Anything we do to rebuild your systems, firewalls, and all, will be too vulnerable with our guy watching. They're definitely keeping tabs on every person and database they demolished, so it would just be an uphill battle to focus on that right now."

"But we need our computers, Parker."

"I know."

"Without them, the whole community is fucked."

Parker sighed frustratedly. "Look, I get it. The hospital said the same thing. I believe it, okay? And I don't want anyone getting hurt. The hacker is just... slippery. Every time I think I'm getting close, they hit me with something new."

"Well, you're not alone anymore, Ms. Rose. I'm on the case, too."

Parker forced a grin. He likely wasn't going to be able to offer her the services she required, but at least she had someone to call should she come face-to-face with the hacker. Hopefully, she'd be able to avoid another violent incident.

"Thanks, Paul."

He clapped his palms and rubbed them together enthusiastically. "So, what's our next move?"

"If we can't rebuild any offline systems, we have to keep the ones we do have afloat, right?"

"Right."

"The fire department supposedly helped you guys with your network protections, which means they're just as susceptible to a hack. Now, if I was trying to torment an entire town, finishing the job of taking out every emergency service would be next on my checklist."

"Which means you gotta go talk with the fire chief."

"Yep."

Paul laughed as he gathered Parker's things, thrusting her overly large jacket and mangled bag into her arms. Unlocking the door, he held it open for her and widely gestured for her to go first. "Good luck with that," he chortled.

"So much for helping me, Paul," Parker chirped.

"Hey, I can't help you with *everything*."
"You're throwing me to the wolves."
"Sometimes, Rose, life just ain't fair."

Chapter 11

It was Parker's turn to bang on somebody's door.

Sometime between Parker arriving at the police station, and the news breaking that another malicious attack had taken place, Jake began to phone Parker. The initial call dropped, and Parker assumed it had been a mistake. He had dialed her accidentally and noticed just before she had the chance to pick up.

And thank God for that, she thought, pulling into her driveway for the first time in days.

But after a brisk shower, a real plate of warm food, and a much-needed change of clothes, Jake was once again on her line. She ignored him intentionally, unwilling to commune with someone who was likely reaching out to see what she didn't know. Or, perhaps, he had garnered some information of his own, and whatever it was contradicted what he thought Parker believed. Little did he know that Parker finally had someone in her corner—Paul would be participating in the dissemination of intel now.

Perhaps that was why, after three more missed calls, she finally picked up. She wanted Jake to know that she had moved on. She had a partner—a cop, no less—and he actually valued the theories that Parker wove. Not only that, she had a renewed sense of purpose with the recent slate of ransoms. The hacker hadn't disappeared with a load of cash, and Parker had a host of avenues to investigate. She wasn't relegated to the same old pointless drivel.

"What do you want?" she murmured into the receiver.

Jake sighed, but he didn't address her with a similar combativeness. Instead, he asked with full sincerity, "Can you come over?"

"Why?" was her short reply.

"We need to talk."

"I think you've said enough."

"No, really, Parker. I want to apologize, and it's only fair to do that to your face."

"Oh…" She was taken aback. "Alright."

So, there she was on his porch, her knuckles colliding with the wood grain he *brought back to life* with several coats of an expensive stain. Another day was coming to an end, the sun drowning below the serene sea, casting the rest of the world in a purple haze. The air was thick with frost, and Parker could see her staccato breaths as they interacted with the frigid atmosphere. She pulled her cardigan tighter around her waist, anxiously looking in Jake's windows for any movement.

She felt as though he was keeping her there. Another twist of the knife, asking her to freeze while he puttered around the house, unbothered by her time or temperament. Parker should have figured this out for a ruse—maybe he was genuine when he called, but after having some hours to think on it, decided against allowing Parker back into his perfect life. She was about to give up when the door cracked open.

"Parker?" Jake whispered.

"Yeah. You didn't hear me?" She couldn't hide the hurt in her voice.

"No, sorry. I was upstairs."

"I've been standing here waiting for you."

"I'm sorry."

For once, she believed him. "Okay."

"Come in," he said and moved so she could enter.

"Thanks," she mumbled.

Pushing through the foyer, Parker kicked off her shoes and tossed her bag on a bench. The house smelled of vanilla candles and floor cleaner. The laundry machines hummed in the background. Dinner had been devoured and put away. The couch had been straightened, the array of pillows and blankets neatly tucked into the corners. Sometimes, Parker was envious of the care Jake applied to his belongings. Inanimate objects received more affection from him than she ever did.

"Please, sit down," he offered, pointing her to the sofa she was slowly coming to resent.

She plopped down on the fluffy cushion but didn't ease into it comfortably. Jake was being too polite and proper; either he wanted something from her, or he was prepping her for the upmost amount of civility. Which meant, funnily enough, that he was going to pepper her with more insults and didn't want to suffer any of the blowback.

"Parker." He touched her thigh and willed her to look at him. The small flames illuminating the space made his eyes appear even richer. His pouty lips were pointed at her sensually. She thought he might lean in to kiss her. She thought he might actually have feelings for her. No—that was just what she wanted, but reality had always ensured that she'd be knocked down a few pegs. "I really want to apologize."

"Why?" she breathed. She was clamming up, her heart telling her to lap up his words without asking further questions. *He meant it; how could he not? Just look at him. Those woeful, innocent eyes...* But Parker was used to always being on the offensive. She had to protect herself, even if that meant refusing the sorrowful artist.

"I've been a real ass," he replied less eloquently.

"Me too," she admitted quietly. It came from her core—sudden, unthinking, and most of all, truthful.

"I've been bashing you for weeks, trying to make you feel bad about yourself and your job. It took me a while to figure out I was just mad at myself. It sucks that I was caught up in my own bullshit for so long that I iced you out, but I wanna make it up to you, okay?"

"What's going on, Jake?"

He sat back on the couch but kept his right hand on her, squeezing her thigh for solace. "I'm just not where I thought I'd be. I know you're going through the same thing. I'm not special. I mean, neither of us are. That's just... the age we're at. But part of me wishes I had done something with the whole murder plot, you know? Actually spun it into something worthwhile for myself. Then again, I feel like those are my old instincts kicking in. The mindset that put me on the map, sure, but also the one that prevented me from having anything real in my life. No friendships, no happiness, no appreciation for anybody or anything. I was miserable in New York." He sighed before continuing, "I was probably miserable as an artist, too."

"Yeah, I know that feeling," Parker added gently. "You're technically doing what you want, and in your case, you're actually successful at it, but it's just not enough. Something nags at you... convinces you that all the people in the world who are better than you are somehow laughing, mocking you for feeling worthwhile, even if only for a minute."

He winced. "That doesn't mean I get to take it out on you, though. You didn't... you didn't do anything wrong. Lashing out at you isn't gonna make me the spectacle ingenue I could have been if I marketed myself right."

Parker shrugged. "I think you made the right choice, not capitalizing off it. Maybe you could have lived with that for a few years, but eventually, you'd have felt guilty about it. Commodifying death isn't exactly a noble thing."

"I know... I know."

"I should apologize, too," Parker offered. She accepted his touch, bringing his fingers into her palm and allowing their warmth to coalesce. "You're not the only one who fucked up. My pride is just as big and just as bruised. I just... I don't want to feel like shit anymore, and the only way I can do that is by pretending that someone else is the villain."

"We've had a tough couple months, Parker."

"Yeah... I think we both deserve some grace. Maybe our bad mouths are neither of our faults."

Jake chuckled. "Okay, maybe that's taking it a tad too far."

"You know what I mean, Jake."

He nodded. "I do."

"Does this mean we're friends again?" She regretted the choice of words as soon as they came out. She watched his kind smile sag, his eyes less hopeful, but only by a small fraction. Plausible deniability.

"Of course," he mumbled. He patted her hand with his free one and then dropped it. They were two separate bodies, again, but at least they were no longer feuding. "Of course..." he repeated.

They stared into the swelling darkness of the home, the sun's light completely erased from the sky and replaced by an all-encompassing navy. Stars weren't visible behind the ever-growing storm clouds.

"It's almost here," Parker announced forebodingly.

"Yeah. It gets bigger every day. They might be calling for an evacuation."

Parker sucked her teeth. "And everybody will be fucked if I don't get my act together."

"Still no progress?" he asked without a hint of smugness in his tone.

"Depends on how you look at it. I was able to figure out that the computer at the hacker's house was the command and control and was hooked up to the library's network. Which means the hacker is sending out signals from one of the devices there. I just haven't figured out which one yet."

"You will."

"I'm not so sure. Those things are ancient and temperamental. Not to mention, the librarian thinks I'm up to no good, but she somehow let a stranger with rotating joke names sign up for multiple memberships and logins."

"Is she in on it?"

Parker smirked. "I considered that for a while—a whole ring of disgruntled desk ladies. Especially when you consider the hospital and how it was the receptionist who clicked on the virus." She paused. "But I should tell you... I'm already working with someone else on the case."

"Oh?"

"Yeah, Paul from the police department."

Jake nearly snorted. "Okay, Parker."

"What?"

"We both know he's…"

"Well-meaning."

"Sure, but—"

"Not all there. I get it. I just, like, don't wanna tell you all these things again if you're not gonna take me or it seriously."

"Parker, I told you I'm sorry about that."

"I know, but maybe I do need to do this alone."

"Already ditching Paul?"

"You know what I mean," Parker grunted.

Jake sighed and inched closer to her. "I want to help. Like, actually help you. I've been thinking about the case, too. The hacker started small and went big, right? Attack the individuals first, and then remove their infrastructure."

"We're on the same page about that."

"They want this whole place to be helpless."

"But why? That's what I can't figure out. People are getting the same threats as the hospital, police department, all that. So wouldn't it have the opposite effect? They're diluting their own message by sending it out to the masses. Clearly, the whole town didn't engage in some fucked up criminal escapade."

"I don't think we can focus on that. Not until we've protected everybody else."

"Won't it make it easier to follow the hacker's trail if we understand why they're doing it in the first place?"

"Do you need a motive to put together that the fire station is the next target?"

Parker grimaced. "No."

"Well, alright then. Let's get going."

***

"Go away," the fire chief hissed.

Parker and Jake had shown up in the middle of the night. The pavement was wet from the humid air, which ravaged the town despite the cold and had come upon the firemen setting up for another drill. The garage doors were wide open, so the pair waltzed in without warning, strolling through the cavernous concrete until they landed upon their victim: fire chief Dale. He was sitting at a desk, perusing papers with his feet up on the table. Half-dressed in his gear, his squad were milling about the garage, poking at hoses and tugging ladders.

"I'm sure you know why we're here," Parker proclaimed coolly.

"Look," Dale grumbled, his thick moustache dancing across his upper lip, "I already told the cop we got this. I don't need backup from some chick and her poet boyfriend."

Both Parker and Jake blushed. "How did he know about that?" Jake muttered under his breath.

"If you're using the same software as the police department, you're gonna get hacked. Simple as, Chief Dale," Parker retorted.

"My boys are smarter than that," Dale insisted. "Besides, we actually monitor our firewalls and network, unlike those buffoons workin' as cops."

"Then have you adapted your systems to account for what's coming?"

"Enough of this horse shit." Dale got up from the desk and loomed over the couple, his eyes glowering with pure detestation. "I know what the fuck I'm talkin' about. I don't need no little girl's help, and I ain't interested in whatever you're selling. Now, get the fuck out."

"Don't talk to her like that," ordered Jake. "We're just trying to protect Watson Bay, something *you* should understand."

"You gotta lot of nerve—"

"And your ego is gonna result in people suffering, Dale. The storm's coming in—"

"I *know* what the fuck I'm doing! I don't need to explain dick to you people. Our system is robust, and we routinely check for viruses and potential hacks. We know our weak spots, and that's why we don't have 'em anymore. We fixed all that shit."

"Fine," Parker snapped. "But don't come crying to me when this place goes under and people are left stranded during the storm."

Parker yanked Jake by the hand and tore out of the garage, trying to keep her head held high so as not to affirm Chief Dale's suspicions about her character. She was not a child, and she certainly wasn't going to behave that way.

Once in the car, Jake asked, "What was that?"

But Parker had pulled out her phone and was already getting to work, locating the fire department's network and worming her way into the code structures. It wasn't hard to do, just as she had failed to advise Dale, and within seconds of punching in commands, she had disabled their internet and seized their data.

"That'll show him," Parker grumbled.

"What did you do?"

"Hacked his arrogant ass."

Her phone was pinging with alerts in a matter of seconds, though. She had been booted from the system, and her malware had been uninstalled. She received a text message.

Dale: You made your point. But I made mine, too. Kicked you out swiftly and without losing anything. Are you happy now?

Parker: Not even remotely. If the ransomware was that simple to decipher, you'd be helping me free the entire goddamn town.

Dale: Stop it, Parker. I'm not interested in your bullshit.

"God, people are annoying," Parker enunciated harshly.

"I know you're gonna kill me for saying this, but maybe it *is* some kind of conspiracy," Jake said slowly.

"I'm not in the mood for this."

"These people obviously have something to hide. Falling for obvious traps, the messages about corruption, and now the fire department withholding help... and for what?"

"I thought motive didn't matter right now?"

"It doesn't, but I'm just trying to show you I'm on your side."

"Yippee," she muttered sarcastically.

"And I think you were onto something. It just doesn't feel right. Either the hacker has supernatural powers, or they're not acting alone."

"Or maybe some of these people deserve it."

Jake shrugged. "Yeah, Parker. Maybe they do."

Chapter 12

Parker held her breath while the phone rang. It was high time she sought advice elsewhere. Though Jake and Paul had both offered their services, and Jake was at least competent and a quick learner, they were out of their league. Another day had passed, and she wasn't any closer to dismantling the ransomware, and the fire department going under was just a ticking time bomb. She told Jake about her plans to return to the library that morning, and while he asked to tag along, Parker knew her muscleman couldn't assist her with this one.

The receiver clicked. "Dad?" Parker called into the phone.

"Parker Posey!" he cheered on the other end.

She blushed at the mention of her long-forgotten childhood nickname. "Hey, Dad," she repeated, unsure of what next to say—how to segue.

"Oh boy, it's so great to hear from you!"

The earnestness of his voice made her feel guilty for dreading this conversation. Maybe if she had reached out more, asking for help wouldn't be such a burden. She frequently declined incoming calls from her parents, citing being swamped with work. It was always a lie—she just didn't want to admit she had nothing going on most days. And when she was on a case, she knew they wouldn't be astounded by it—the exception should have been the rule at her age.

"I missed you," he continued to coo.

"I missed you, too."

"So! What's up with you? How's my girl?"

"Um... I'm alright," she wavered.

"That makes sense. I heard there's supposed to be a gnarly storm coming your way. Why don't you come visit your mother and I? Wait it out somewhere safe?"

"Well, uh, that's actually why I called."

"I thought you'd say that. We already have the guest bedroom set up for you, and your mother will head out to the grocery store today to pick up all your favorite things. What are you eating these days?"

"No, Dad. I didn't mean I was coming. I, um, well, I need to get people back online before the storm hits."

"Oh," he uttered softly and then went quiet. Parker thought the call had dropped, straining her ears until she finally heard the wisps of his breathing. "You're still working for that town, huh?"

"Yeah, I got a better gig."

He scoffed. "Not possible in Watson Bay."

"Oh, come on Dad, you knew I was here when you picked up, hence you offering me to stay with you guys."

"Remaining where you are while you make plans to leave is totally fine. But choosing to put down roots there?" he grunted.

"I'm doing good for myself, Dad. And the whole dang town. There's this hacker—"

"When are you going to strive for greater things, my girl?"

"I'm doing exactly what you taught me."

"You should be venturing around the world. I heard kids your age usually choose to go backpacking through Europe or Asia. I'd prefer it if you toured Europe. I have a lot more questions about their history—"

"I'm doing good work in Watson Bay. I'm not interested in leaving. Not yet, anyways."

"So, there's hope?"

Parker sighed deeply. "Please, Dad... I'm doing my best. And even then, I actually like what I've got going on here."

"Which is?"

"I'm a private investigator."

"Small potatoes," he grumbled.

"You're not the first person to say that to me."

"Well, good. That means you're talking to someone with some sense."

"Please," she pleaded again, "Watson Bay is in a lot of trouble. I just need your advice, okay? That's all I'm calling about. Not a lecture. Not to hear how disappointed you are about my choices—"

"Okay, okay," he conceded. "I'm sorry, Parker Posey. I just... I care a lot about you. I see how talented and bright you are. I don't want to be the only one who does."

"You're not," she fibbed. "I can promise you that."

"Alright, then," he replied, softening even further. "What do you need?"

Parker took a great inhale and then said, "A hacker has been terrorizing the whole town. And I mean everyone. They started by locking a couple doctors' phones with ransomware and then moved on to the hospital. They wiped everything, Dad, and pulled a whole bunch of machines offline. Then, they went after the police station, and I'm certain the fire department is next."

"Hm... you know how to hack 'em right back, Parker. We've been over this kind of code disruption a million times."

"I know, Dad, but this hacker is like really advanced. Except they're using the most outdated computers they could find. Older than the ones we still have at home. So, I'm at a loss."

"Well, you know what computer the virus is spreading from?"

"In a way. They've got a command and control located at an abandoned house out in Thorton and have connected everything they're doing to the library's network. I think the true source is there, but when I tried to break into the mainframe a couple days ago, the system was too slow for me to make any real progress. Whatever the hacker has buried within the software is like impossible to retrieve."

"Nothing's impossible, dear."

"I mean, I know that *theoretically*, but I'm struggling. Hard. And I didn't think this would be an issue for me. Like you said, 'We've done this a million times.'"

"So, this hacker has got a full-blown operation happening... to take down Watson Bay?" her dad asked incredulously.

"Yeah."

"Why would somebody wanna do that?"

"I dunno, Dad. The ransoms are all sent with the same accusation of a crime, but they don't say what. Just that everyone has committed some kind of atrocity."

"Who do they think they are, the Zodiac killer?"

Parker chortled. "Thank God nobody's died yet."

"But with this storm coming..."

"Exactly."

"Alright... this may not be the life I imagined for you, but I see why you've taken this up as a cause. I respect that, Parker."

"You do?"

"I do," he replied airily.

"So you'll help me?"

"Of course, my girl. Do you have a piece of paper and a pen ready? You'll want to take this down."

***

Margaret was hesitant to let Parker back into the computer room. They held each other's gazes for too long, caught in a gun draw without any ammo. Parker figured her appearance wasn't doing her any favors—she certainly looked like somebody up to no good in her oversized black hoodie and baggy sweats. But the librarian couldn't deny her access to something without just cause, and Parker had a mouth on her, that was certain. Either allow the girl to fiddle with the computers or have the denial haunt Margaret for the rest of her life. In the end, she scornfully gave Parker a login, hoping that any minor annoyances she derived from today's experience would far outweigh whatever nonsense Parker could produce in the long run.

Seated at a randomly selected computer, Parker no longer cared if the librarian pried into her business—she was the one trying to save Watson Bay, and she didn't feel the need to hide that fact from some bored lady behind a desk. With her father's instructions neatly splayed before her on the unwrinkled sheet of notepaper, Parker got to work.

His advice had been to scale it back. An outdated computer meant outdated codes. There weren't as many moving parts back in the day—fewer networks, software possibilities, and potential calibrations. The infrastructure of the machine itself was more rudimentary than a modern device. Parker was trying to apply encryptions that worked on hardware worth thousands of dollars to a computer that didn't recognize such commands. Her shortcuts weren't adapted to the make and model of what she was presently dealing with.

No matter how obvious her dad's suggestions had been, they began to take shape on the screen. First, she was within the administrative functions in mere seconds rather than hours. Then, she was reading the strands of code that determined the computer's functionality, sending out signals with short keystrokes and antiquated terms. It was all too simple, which Parker loathed.

She always had the perception that for something to be worth it, it had to be exorbitantly difficult. She was never good at anything because of this—no hobby could be fruitful if she accepted shortcuts were part of the deal. Baking didn't please her when an array of 20 ingredients and hours of fussy labor wasn't involved. A tasty loaf of bread didn't mean anything, didn't make her accomplished if she hadn't even kneaded it routinely for days on end. She wanted to take up painting but couldn't stomach starting as a beginner, coloring within predetermined lines and following clear instructions in order to make something beautiful. If she couldn't do it right the first time—if she couldn't *be* the only one to do it at all—then it was a waste. Unfortunately, she had applied that logic to the hacker's game.

Parker was certain they had to be a mastermind and that only someone as equally intelligent could bring them down. She was more focused on impressing people with her intricate codes and unique capabilities than on genuinely understanding what was before her. The hacker was simply using a system of computers that nobody would think to look at: It had nothing to do with complexity, endurance, or inhuman brilliance. Convenience was probably the better word. Perhaps the hacker was older and therefore used machinery they were used to. They had access to a free public space, and so they took advantage of it.

"Aha," Parker said reflexively.

Miraculously, the device she had chosen was indeed wired by the hacker. She found the embedded instructions to disable and harvest data from the already targeted IP addresses. With a few more clicks, she had disabled it.

She sat back for a moment, proud of the work she had done despite its unsophistication. Tempted, she reached for her phone to give Jake the good news, but she thought about it for a moment and decided an attack this large likely wasn't coming from two devices. She scoured the computer's software for clues as to where the other malicious devices were positioned but couldn't gain any insight. She'd have to restart the process over and over again, clearing every machine in the room before she could resolve that she had completed her task. Imploring herself not to run wild with her minor success, Parker was back at the librarian's desk demanding a new login.

"No," Margaret refuted.

"Give me a break," Parker moaned.

"I told you this last time: one computer. You get one, and you stick with it."

"I think we both know I'm not writing an essay in there."

"That just affirms my position—"

"Listen, I'm working for the police department, and it's imperative that I use these—"

"Oh?" Margaret seemed unfazed by the claim. "We're closing soon, anyway."

Parker, confused, looked at the large clock on the wall behind Margaret's head. "It's only three."

"We close at three-thirty on Saturdays."

Baffled, Parker struggled to adjust to the information. "Okay, then I still have half an hour. That's enough time for me to scan at least a couple more computers."

"For what?"

"The hacker—"

"Enough of this," Margaret shot back as she rolled her eyes. "People are acting like we're under siege. So a couple morons visited the wrong websites—big whoop. But this isn't a villainous plan to take over the town."

"You won't be saying that when the library goes down."

"It would never go down."

Parker sighed. Why was everyone insistent on repeating the same dreadful lines? "You're not the first one to say that," she replied, echoing her own routine conversation points. "When a library gets held for ransom like that, all of your employees are at risk. Their information is stolen, your jobs become moot, and now you have to rebuild your entire schema for this building, your shelves, all of it, because you refused to listen to me. Do you wanna go down with the ship or something?"

"I'm no martyr, but my shift is about to be over, and I'd really like to go home."

"Me too, but there's a storm coming in, and I need to stop—"

"I said no, and that's final, Ms. Rose."

What was preventing Parker from breaking into the machines of her own volition? She didn't have to keep asking for permission. Frustrated, she marched over to the computer room and began her own pillage, selecting another computer to dismantle and readying her codes to infiltrate the archaic system. She was sick of rolling over for these people. They didn't want to listen? Fine. But she didn't have to let everyone suffer just because some residents were too proud or spiteful to let her do her goddamn work.

But then the lights shut off, and all the computers went black. "Margaret!" Parker barked.

"Whoops," came the librarian's voice. "Looks like we close at three today."

"Do you always flip the breaker when you lock up?"

Margaret was hovering by the entrance, a smirk plastered on her red lips, which were aggravatingly visible even in the dimness. "Always. Now, please, let me walk you out."

Gritting her teeth, Parker unceremoniously grabbed her things and blew past the arrogant librarian into the overcast afternoon. A chill went down her spine as the wind swept across the parking lot, kicking up debris and whipping it around the concrete wasteland. The clouds looked no better—they were gaining mass, hovering over the town like a murderous dome. Things were about to devolve into chaos, and for some reason, nobody was willing to stop it.

Chapter 13

"So," Dale began gruffly, "we've been hacked."

"Shocker," Parker responded sarcastically.

"Was this another one of your little tricks? You know, to prove something?"

"My God, Dale, I have better things to do."

Moments after Parker had left the library, she'd received threatening messages from Chief Dale insisting that she meet him at the fire station. Predictably, the hacker had infiltrated their system, ostensibly learning it after attacking the police department, and had stolen all of their data. They were being held for a ransom of 30 million in Bitcoin, and Dale was perplexed by the whole ordeal. As if Parker hadn't warned him about it. As if this couldn't have been avoided if he had just heeded her advice. But those weren't points worth harping on now. The damage had already been done.

"I hope you know you weren't the first person I called," Dale added. "Just because I was overconfident doesn't mean you're somehow the default expert."

"I kind of am," Parker said as she reclined, soaking up every moment of Dale's pathetic show.

"Our firewalls didn't fail. We have several protocols to manage this sort of thing—all of which alerted us to the hack—and nobody is responsible for letting the virus in."

"No fishy emails?"

"None."

"And you're sure your cohort is telling the truth?"

Dale sighed. "Positive. I can track all of their internet and computer usage. I don't know how the ransomware made it through."

"The hacker probably didn't need an in this time."

"What do you mean?"

"Whoever they are, they've learned enough about all of Watson Bay's networks and codes to just open whatever door they want. You didn't update your safety net after the police department was compromised, and the hacker had already pinpointed the cracks in your system."

"It's a robust—"

"I wormed my way through the firewall, too. I didn't need to prey on somebody letting me in for that to happen. But the hacker needed less time than me to plant their malware. A quick reaction to disable my benign and aimless attack means nothing against someone who knows what they're doing. The hacker was on a foolproof mission."

"You're right," Chief Dale admitted, even if only to placate Parker. "I guess I'm just... cocky."

"You can say that again."

Dale scowled. "Well, are you gonna help us restore our systems or what?"

"I'm working on it," she replied vaguely.

Now it was Dale's turn to browbeat her. "You've been on the case for weeks."

"It's a difficult one. You just found this out yourself."

He chortled, leaning over the desk and resting his large forearms against the wood grain. "I didn't have such a large head start, Parker. And I sure as hell didn't take money for services I couldn't make good on."

"I think the police force would have something different to say," she rebuked as sharply as she could manage, but she had to confess that he had her cornered. Would she even have been able to protect the department from the inevitable onslaught? It wasn't like she had an exact code or equation that would halt the hacker in their tracks. Nothing tried and true. She had ideas from her father, but they were still scribbles on a page, yet to be applied to anything in the real world where it mattered. Stopping a computer wasn't the same as building a line of defense against the machine.

"I need my systems back online before this damn storm," he snarled.

"So does everybody else. I'm working on it."

"That's the best you got?"

"That's all anyone's got," she answered resolutely. And it was the truth. They were all winging it against a nameless, faceless entity hell-bent on destroying their community. It wasn't much faith to cling to, but it had to be enough for now. Enough to face the storm without crumbling.

However, this sentiment didn't resonate with the rest of the population. Dale sent her on her way, muttering under his breath about inefficiency and human error, but he had at least tepidly agreed to trust her. She would come back to him with news, results, something, in a few days. The people currently lined up outside her house, though, no longer had the patience for Parker's investigation.

She couldn't park in her own driveway, which was flooded with all sorts of Watson Bay folks. Their faces were so clouded with misery and anguish that they may as well have been holding picket signs demanding Parker's head. She knew that as the weather ramped up, people would begin to get anxious, but she didn't expect an all-out revolt. Leaving her car, headlights on, by the side of the road, Parker charged up the driveway and approached the mob waiting for her arrival. She attempted to walk with her chest puffed and head high, but the moment eyes interlocked with hers, she felt her false confidence waver.

"There she is!" someone shouted from the depths of the crowd.

"Liar!" yelled another.

Parker held up her hands, a bullfighter trying to carefully evade the animal's horns. "Whoa, guys," she replied lamely. "What's going on?"

"You know damn well what's going on!" a voice cried.

"I don't," Parker insisted, though it didn't take a genius to figure out what was transpiring before her.

Maxine emerged from the thicket like a prophet, the waves parting for her as she mustered up the courage to stand up to Parker's tyranny. "We need our phones back," she demanded, her tone wavering.

Heads nodded, voices carried, and eyes shone on her like a million violent flashlights. The moment she dreaded was finally here; the confessional forced out of her by a swarm of frightened people. Parker's heart smashed against her chest cavity, and her face felt like it was on fire. She knew there'd be a confrontation when she made her presence known, but for some reason, thinking about it wasn't quite the same as being in the middle of it. She was unprepared to face their wrath, to stutter and fumble while she sloppily explained she was behind schedule. Not because of her incompetence but because of her self-sabotaging inner turmoil. She had prioritized her bad feelings over investigating a genuine crime. Had she even opened their devices, scrolled through their contents, and accrued new information from the stockpile? She couldn't remember, which meant she likely hadn't. What the fucked had she been doing with her time? That was what they would ask her. That was what she had to repent for.

"You'll get them back," she promised, the words empty as her mind reeled with the truth.

"When?" Maxine persisted.

"Soon!"

"Bullshit!" someone bellowed in the distance.

"Yeah, we've been waiting forever," another corroborated.

"These things take time," Parker assured them, "and there are a lot of you and only one of me!"

"So, you're not capable of taking this on," replied Maxine. "You haven't even been back to the hospital since I called you in. People need treatment."

"I know!" Parker wailed, her emotions catching up to her and disrupting her facade. "I'm trying, you guys."

"Are you?" asked Maxine.

"Yes! I promise! This is a really difficult case."

"The storm is here, and we can't be without our phones. I'm not gonna be stranded in my house because of you."

"But your phone won't work," Parker maintained.

"We'll fix 'em ourselves," offered the woman standing beside Maxine. She had electric red hair, bold eyeliner, and a face that could have been either 20 or 40. She was nestled in an oversized black puffer jacket and pulled a pack of cigarettes from her pocket while she spoke. "I may be no genius, but I'm sure I can figure it out. I solve problems all day long as a nurse."

"These aren't the same problems."

"Sure they are," the red-haired woman said cavalierly and took a drag of her newly lit cigarette. "Run some tests, take some notes, match the evidence to the cause."

"But we don't know what the cause is. I've been trying to tell everybody: The hacker is five steps ahead. Tracing their output from your phones means nothing if I can't follow their movements, and there are all these decoys, dead ends, fake names... It's not as simple as hitting a few buttons and disabling the ransomware."

"We'll pay the ransom then," chimed Maxine. "Maybe it won't be possible for the hospital to swing that, but if it comes down to saving the lives of me and my kids, I'll pay just about anything."

"Besides," added the red-haired lady, "can't we just warn our banks about this? Like, rig up some sort of fraudulent transaction to lure the hacker in, and once he thinks he has my money, I just yank it back?"

"You guys don't know what you're doing any more than I do," Parker growled childishly.

"I like my odds better relying on myself."

"Banks don't lend you Bitcoin, so you can entrap a hacker."

"Who cares? I lent you money, and nothing came of it. If I can take the loss, so can a bank."

"I didn't rip anyone off."

"We're not here to bleed you dry, Parker," said Maxine. "We just want our phones back."

The crowd was rushing around her, their expectant expressions applying pressure to Parker's fragile esteem. She knew it wasn't in their best interest to give them false hope, to allow them to spend money they didn't have, and to mess with software they didn't understand. But she couldn't make them see that they were no safer trying to go this alone—something she had trouble digesting herself, too. In her desperate attempts to be the hero of Watson Bay, she had only pushed her community further into precariousness. And now they were at their limit, no longer trusting her alleged expertise. She wanted to stand up for herself, to finally put her money where her mouth was, but she couldn't blame them for not taking the bait.

Parker attempted to form words, sounds, utterances, but her mind drew a blank. Her tongue didn't want to snap just as much as her heart didn't want to continue to lead these people astray. Bowing her head, she solemnly marched through the crowd, surprised murmurs erupting at her defeat. As though they didn't anticipate she'd give up so easily. Part of her worried that the reputation she'd garnered wasn't as positive as she had spun it to herself a million times over. That being sassy and strong-willed wasn't something to be proud of if it meant everyone assumed she was stubborn rather than rightfully determined.

She unlocked her front door, looking back at the mass she had accumulated, and wordlessly gestured for them to wait. Without bothering to turn on the lights, she trudged over to the piles of devices, most of them now contained within plastic bins, and hauled one batch to the door.

"Jessica!" she hollered, waving around a compact laptop.

A blond woman rushed to Parker's side, quickly evaluated the brand logo and scratches along the exterior, and accepted the offering. Parker guiltily watched as Jessica skipped down the driveway, already a victim of an email scam and likely to burn herself a second time without the proper knowledge to protect herself.

"You guys can still call me for advice," Parker announced. "I don't want you to do anything stupid."

Surprisingly, nobody gave her flack for the remark. One by one, Parker listed off names and dolled out devices. The throngs of people dwindled, and tensions eased when it became clear that Parker was at least holding one promise. There was no game being played here—they wanted their property back, so she obliged. Hours had passed before the final exchange—which was received with a curt grin but disapproving head shake—and Parker was finally alone.

Shutting the door, Parker sank to the ground, her knees quaking while the reality of the situation set in. It was always one step forward and two steps back with her, and she always failed to see it coming. She never changed her behavior and never accepted anyone's advice until it was too late. She was just a spitting image of Dale, though less abrasive, and it was a wonder she had made it this far in life with her one-track mind.

Parker pulled out her phone, the only remaining untainted device in Watson Bay, and dialed the sole person she wanted to talk to. "Jake?" she moaned into the receiver.

"Uh oh," he replied smoothly. "You don't sound good."

"I fucked up," she whimpered, releasing the emotions that had been pent up inside.

"What happened? I'm sure it's not as bad as you think."

"I lost every single cell phone, computer, tablet... everything the hacker had disabled."

"How?" he asked, his voice still unrelentingly even.

"Everyone demanded their shit back, that's how."

He clicked his tongue. "Well... did you really need it?"

"I don't know. Maybe. Probably, yeah."

"I'm not so sure about that, Parker. We have a lot of leads on the hacker, and none of that came from somebody's phone."

"Because I hadn't properly looked," she admitted. "I got sidetracked. Again. Like I always do."

"You were following newer, better leads. You got nothing out of Dr. Marshal's and Ang's stuff, right?"

"Right," she replied meekly.

"So what made you think someone else's device would be any different?"

"A bigger pool to choose from, I guess. More variables and possibilities."

"Variables for *what*, though? So, you found the source of the virus, now what? You would have been right back at the hacker's house, rifling through that mysterious computer. Same sequence, different order."

"Are you sure, Jake? Like, you're not just saying that to pacify me?"

"I swear, Parker. I mean it."

She took a deep breath, her fingers mindlessly playing with a loose thread on the seam of her jeans. The lights remained off in Parker's melancholic stupor, and suddenly, the serenity of her home had vanished. She didn't want to be alone.

"Can you come over?" she found herself asking into the receiver.

"Of course." His cadence was smooth. Buttery. "I'm on my way."

Chapter 14

Anonymous: Fun game you're playing.

Parker stared at the screen blankly.

Anonymous: Very moronic, though.

She was neither afraid nor elated. She had to expect this outcome after what she'd done, but it still felt a little surreal. As the days wore on and the hacker's scheme continued to devour Watson Bay, the person behind the torment took on a mythical aura. Nobody knew their name or gender, though most people resorted to referring to them as *he*. They seemingly lived away from the people, and yet they were everywhere, a God with an overactive eye and too much time on their hands. Sometimes, Parker felt like she was hallucinating them, unable to put together a picture because of the insurmountable dead ends and wondering whether or not she was following real clues or making up evidence just to suit her narrative. To justify the time she had spent on such a trial.

This had led her back to the hacker's alleged house. That command and control computer beckoned her, pleaded with her to finally infiltrate its systems. Jake stood behind her, making good on his promise to support her without wavering, but still nervous about what peril she'd find herself in this time. She was entirely forthcoming about her plan—install a virus on the device to draw out the hacker—but she could tell Jake was silently wishing this would be another bust. Her fingers quaked as she typed in the code, lacing it through the system and effectively sending off an alert to the person behind the machine if there ever was one. She could still feel the dryness of her mouth and the cold sweat behind her neck as she boldly put herself in the middle of a hostile crisis. Fortunately or unfortunately, things had worked in Parker's favor.

Parker wondered how long she should wait before responding. The hacker was a passionate person, that was apparent. These crimes were ones of retribution, unceremoniously doled out to the masses as a form of punishment for a perceived slight against the assailant. They were not genuinely seeking a pot of gold but rather wanted to put the community in a precarious place. Forcing their hand at an apology, a dramatic plea for forgiveness, that was worth more to the hacker than any Bitcoin. If anything was going to set the villain off, it would be messing with their precious and highly curated blueprint. A wedge so hard to ignore that in their fury, perhaps they might trip up and make a mistake.

Anonymous: Don't ignore me.

Parker smirked. Already, her theories were unfolding—she just had to up the ante.

Anonymous: I can see your screen. I know you're looking at me.

Parker: Can you see me picking my nose, too?

Anonymous: Of course, you don't want to take this seriously.

Parker: Pretending to be the Joker now? I didn't know I was at Comic-Con.

Parker: You know that's for children and arrested development adults, right?

Anonymous: I'm not as stupid as you. I'm not taking the bait.

Parker: I'm not sure what you're referring to.

She chuckled to herself as she locked her phone, turning it off for the evening and forcing the hacker to stew in her blasé responses. Obviously, this person didn't want to be ignored and wouldn't react well to it. She figured she'd wake up to a slew of messages, but that would only serve as more material for her to draw upon. She had to keep them hooked, playing into her devices while she worked covertly behind the scenes to track their location. Perhaps she couldn't do it through a foreign entity, but her own cell phone? She knew that software inside and out. Regardless of how intelligent the hacker believed themself to be, Parker was efficient with modern technology. She'd have this sucker in no time.

***

"You think you're clever, Parker Rose. *Oh no, my computer has a little virus on it, what ever will I do*? All you've done is make an enemy out of me. You haven't stopped anything, though. In fact, now I have a little hobby while I wait for the grand finale to take off. How lucky am I? If anything, you should be patting yourself on the back for driving the final nail in the coffin of Watson Bay. I'll be talking to you again soon. Bye bye!"

The dial tone replaced the masculine voice that had snarled into her messages. Instead of a barrage of texts, the hacker had opted to make themself heard in an undeniable way. The words should have chilled her to the core, yes, but she was more invested in the tone itself. Had the hacker altered their voice in any meaningful way? Had they used AI in order to trick Parker into falling for another false identity, or were they merely ripping off part of the mask, enabling her to gain insight into their age, makeup, and accent?

She sent the voicemail to Jake, who agreed that nothing sounded odd or stilted. There weren't weird robotic tinges to the vowels and hollow reverberations that skewed the believability of the speaker. It was, hopefully, all too real.

"Can we quantify this as a mistake?" Parker asked Jake over the phone.

"I'm not sure," he confessed. "He's pretty adamant that you won't catch him."

"I know, but when people are full of themselves, they usually arrogantly assume they can fuck up, and nobody will realize. Maybe even intentionally fuck up. Or he's so goddamn smug he thinks he doesn't have to hide anything and will still walk away clean."

Jake paused. "You think he's listening in right now?"

Parker paled. That was a reality. Just what she had accused the hacker of, she was so bold in her assertion that she would wrangle him; she was dashing right into his trap by blabbing about her ideas on the very device the hacker had certainly tapped. She decided to lean into it, though. What did she have to lose? He had her name, address, and whatever valuable materials she kept on her devices. This was a consequence of her big-brained strategy, and she couldn't clam up now.

"So what? He thinks he knows what I want; there's no harm in confirming it. He can trace me; I can trace him."

"Yeah, but... you shouldn't *tell* him—"

"What other purpose did I have when I messed with his computer? We're both willingly in the situation now. Might as well play fair."

Predictably, the hacker made himself known at the first opportunity.

Anonymous: You overestimate your abilities, Rose. I've looked into all your work, and I must say, it's quite juvenile. Shoddy stuff.

Parker: I tracked you once; I can do it again.

Anonymous: But I wasn't hiding my footprint. It's not an accomplishment when I led you to the water.

Parker: You keep talking to me, jackass. I'll have your location pinged in a heartbeat.

Anonymous: Oh really? Try doing it without a phone.

The screen went dark. *Shit.* Scurrying across the living room, she flipped open her laptop and furiously typed in her password. She was disabling the hack on her phone when her computer shut down just the same. But suddenly, her cell was alive again, the hacker shooting off messages with one hand and ravaging her devices with the other.

Anonymous: See?

Anonymous: And those aren't the only things I can command.

Her microwave was rotating, her kettle was boiling, and her speakers were blasting. All these pieces of tech she felt so proud about owning because they had Bluetooth or smart interfaces were now shouting at her in their mechanical cadences. Her vacuum cleaner swiveled around the floor, no doubt the hacker trying to gain intel on the layout of her home. She stamped her feet down on the machine like it was a bug she could squash.

Anonymous: How stupid can you be?

Anonymous: Letting all these cameras into your home.

Her heart was racing. Cameras? What cameras? She looked between her phone and laptop and connected the dots. Slamming her computer shut and pressing her cell against her chest, she scanned the rest of the house. Was the microwave somehow bugged? How would a surveillance system be implemented in such a device? It was like all her fears over inadequacy were catching up. She couldn't evade him. She couldn't think fast enough. Within seconds, he had her afraid to use her phone, the very thing she needed to track his movements. To find out who he was. No, she couldn't do this again.

Parker: You can't intimidate me.

Anonymous: Is that what you think I'm after?

Parker: What are you after?

And then the chaos halted. Parker was in the eye of the storm, surrounded by the carnage and yet somehow briefly immune. She was due for another torrent, and perhaps this pivot was the smartest thing the hacker had done. Though she was back on her computer, hastily punching in codes in order to deconstruct his messages and find their source, she couldn't help but feel watched. Pursued. Like her cursor was being puppeteered somewhere just out of reach.

"I assumed these consequences," she reminded herself in a whisper. "I knew this was going to happen." She bit her tongue. Even this bout of weakness, of questioning, was fodder for the hacker.

Jake: Come over, Parker

She read the message, glaring at the lettering like it was carved into a tombstone. He was the only one who had yet to be brought into the hacker's world of terror, and now Parker was putting a target on his back once more by allowing such obvious and easily delineated communications to reach her.

Without thinking, she packed up her things, tucking all of her tainted technology underneath couch cushions where they could no longer monitor the inside of her home and unplugging everything that couldn't be stowed. With her car keys in hand, she bumbled out the door to alert Jake.

***

"Okay, good," Jake breathed when Parker was standing at his doorstep. "That was fast, too. I thought I'd have to beg."

"I mean... I'm not *staying*," she fibbed.

Jake tugged her arm, softly propelling her into his foyer. He stripped her of her jacket, knocked on her toes until she took off her shoes, and dragged her by her limp wrists into the living room. A fire was gently ebbing on the hearth, and had Parker not feared for Jake's safety, she would have obliged his warm invitation.

"Yes, you are," he finally counteracted.

"Look, I'll fill you in on everything that happened today, but—"

"But nothing. That freak knows where you live."

"He knows where you live, too. He knows everything about all of us. But just because he has an address doesn't mean he's gonna come barging in to kill me."

"Come on, it can't be just murder that you take seriously."

"He sounds old. His voice is all gravelly. I bet I could take him in a fight. Besides, if he was a mastermind killer, he wouldn't be hiding behind a screen."

Jake sighed. "What happened?"

Parker fumbled, her fingers reaching up to her face as if to trace the details on her skin that gave her away.

"I know you pretty well, Parker. I know when you're exaggerating to hide the truth, which is that you're scared shitless."

"I'm not..."

"It's okay. Your plan didn't backfire, but it's not going great, either."

"Yeah, but I can't let that stop me. I left all my tech at my place."

"Were you getting anything out of it?"

Parker fidgeted, shifting her weight from leg to leg as she struggled to find the correct answer. The one that would preserve her ego and reassure Jake. That was a loss, though. "No," she admitted quietly. "I thought I was finally onto something this time. Like I wasn't all talk."

"You knew he was faster than you."

"At outdated machines, not *modernity*."

"But you said it yourself already: He has your information. He has mine. Nothing was private, even without him directly interacting with you. It was only a matter of time before something like this happened."

"And I expedited it for myself. Which I'm doing for you right now, too, by even letting you text me. Now he knows we're in cahoots."

Jake rolled his eyes coyly. "Sure, whatever, Parker. That's a problem for tomorrow. Tonight, though, we're both safe here."

"He said there are cameras in my home, and I just can't believe I didn't realize that. I surround myself with all these machines, thinking I'm their master, and I'm brought back down to earth time and time again. I can't have a win for more than a fucking day!"

"He's trying to intimidate you."

"He said he wasn't. And when I asked what he *did* want with me, he didn't respond. Or maybe he has by now. But I fled. I cannot stop being the fucking coward, Jake. I mean, I'm tired of this cycle. I'm tired of being up one minute and down the next. Aren't you exhausted just knowing me?"

He stood up from the sofa, meeting her eyes and cupping her damp cheeks in his hands. He stared at her longingly, tilting their chins until it seemed like their lips would meet. "Shh," he lulled, "I'm not tired of you."

"But at one point you were," she pestered, adrenaline fuelling her frazzled state.

"Parker... we talked about this."

"I know."

"I like you. You're my..." he faltered. "*Friend*."

The moment was broken, just as it was when Parker uttered the condemned word. He dropped his hands, and they were left to stand in their discomfort, unsure of how to continue after such a charged encounter. So, Jake took the lead, motioning for her to follow him down the hall toward the guest bedroom. He'd already made it up, pulling back the freshly cleaned sheets so she could hop in right away. He put towels on the chair in the corner, showed her how to get the hot water to the perfect temperature in the shower, and offered to get her pajamas from his closet. She had no choice but to accept, having shown up with nothing but her person.

Wearing his T-shirt and flannels, Parker got under the covers, ravenously inhaling the scent of his detergent. She thought of his hands as they moved across the fabric, lovingly splaying it for her, making sure it was without blemish. Part of her was wounded that he hadn't made a pass, taking the leap and offering up his own bed for comfort, but Parker had contributed to her estranged sleeping arrangement.

When the quietness of the home settled in, and she could no longer heed the sounds of Jake turning off the lights and taking one last tour of the property, she was once more filled with unease. The alarm clock on the dresser was a problem, and so was the TV hung on the wall, capable of scanning the room for consumers to target ads to. The hacker could easily be watching, waiting for the moment when her body ceased to fight to stay awake. Who knew what was in Jake's room, precariously placed without concern and ripe for the hacker's viewing. Should she warn him?

Sometime during her tussling, however, she managed to fall asleep.

Chapter 15

Parker peered into the window of her own house, her hands cupped around the frosted glass, blurring the contents of the living room with her looming shadow. Jake had driven her here early in the morning, desperate to ease Parker's mind. She had been up for hours, fretting over what could be waiting for her and insisting that Jake continuously check his phone to make sure the hacker hadn't moved onto him. She reminded him once more that he was likely the last person standing in Watson Bay, and she didn't think it was a coincidence that he was the only outsider, too. His hands, obviously, were clean of whatever blood the hacker felt had been shed. Did that make him immune to the hacker's streak of destruction? Was he to be salvaged from the chaos? Jake thought she was going overboard, but Parker couldn't help but mull over the connection between his short history with the town and the hacker's insistence that the people were all demonic. That they had done something they must pay for.

"All clear, Parker," Jake informed her as he emerged from around the back of the house.

It was another sunless day, and the morning dew had crystallized on blades of grass and leaves hanging from branches. The air was so thick with water that it felt as though they were standing in a ceaseless, invisible shower, their skin sweating with the ephemeral liquid. *This was the kind of weather monsters always struck during*, Parker noted. There were many dense pockets of fog, cement was already slick, meaning blood would blend right in, and the horizon glared at the town forebodingly. Nothing looked or felt good. The atmosphere made Parker all the more apprehensive.

"We just have to..." she began, struggling to speak through her ragged breaths. "We just have to check my phone."

He nodded, running his fingers through the ends of Parker's hair. "It'll be fine," he promised. "We just have to be smart about it. That's all."

"But I haven't been *smart* thus far," she insisted stubbornly.

"Yes, you have. I'm not sure what else you think you were supposed to do. But the hacker is overwhelming, omnipresent... it's bizarre. And nobody else has stood up to him or figured out how to. It's just been you, Parker."

She opened her mouth to retort, but he silenced her calmly with his raised fingers. Taking her by the hand, a habit he was forming and one that Parker didn't want him to become aware of and stop, he gently dragged her to the front door. He sternly waited while she unlocked the knob, relieved that it hadn't been tampered with, and crossed the threshold into the empty house.

"Look okay so far?" Jake asked, his voice echoing across the peculiar landscape of Parker's home.

"I think so," she replied.

Her laptop and other screens were still underneath couch cushions, seemingly turned off and cold to the touch. The appliances she had unplugged remained still and unused, waiting for her to breathe new life into them with a jolt of electricity. She checked the bedrooms, the attic, and the bathroom, all before she could muster the courage to flip over her phone. Jake believing in her should have been enough to embolden her—wasn't that what she wanted? Someone in her corner? Especially someone as beautiful and kind as Jake. Yet she remained tepid, afraid, constantly waiting for the other shoe to drop.

She reached down and grabbed the phone.

Anonymous: Nowhere in Watson Bay is safe.

Parker inhaled sharply. Jake rushed to her side, eager to see what was the matter. He gazed over her shoulder, taking a peek at the bright screen.

Anonymous: Not for you.

Anonymous: Not for anyone.

"I told you I was gonna make you a target," Parker announced coolly.

Jake unlocked his device and after a quick glance, shoved it back in his pocket. "I'm still good. But that doesn't matter—what matters is that we protect *you*. Not me."

"How?"

Jake brushed his own hair, pushing back the black strands roughly while he thought. "I don't know, Parker. I don't like that you're in the middle of this..."

"I thought you said you'd support me—"

"I *do*. I am. It's just... I'm out of my element, too, you know."

Parker and Jake took a deep breath in tandem, their eyes boring into each other as they derived consolation from their mirrored movements.

"We should take this whole mission offline," Parker suggested suddenly. Jake shot her a quizzical look, so she continued, "Well, we both agree I haven't exactly ensnared the hacker with one of my brilliant schemes. When it comes to technology, this guy is everywhere. He knows what to look for, how to look for it, and importantly, it feels like he's tracking my keystrokes meticulously. I'm not gonna be able to find a single computer or cellphone in this town that he isn't already monitoring."

"But all these attacks are happening, you know, in the internet sphere or whatever," Jake countered.

"This guy exists beyond a software, though. Something happened to him in the outside world that made him this way. It has to be tangible, Jake." She lowered her voice, "I'm not trying to pick at old wounds, but I think we need to reconsider whether or not someone actually deserves all this. Maybe even the whole community. This guy has been slighted for real."

Jake bit his lip, but his expression remained open. He wasn't about to lash out at Parker. Instead, he replied, "I may not like agreeing with you on this one, but I can't argue that something had to have happened. I mean, it all started with the nurses, right?"

"The doctors. Marshal and Ang. Then it was the rest of the healthcare workers, then the whole hospital, and it's been a domino effect ever since."

"You said it first, but maybe there was some kind of medical malpractice. Maybe it was Dr. Marshal who hurt the hacker. But a citywide cover-up? I'm gonna need to chew on that for a while."

"It only sounds absurd because we haven't found any proof of it yet. I mean, yeah, I can't really think of some terrible crime that everyone partook in, but maybe that's because we don't have the context for it. We need to find a source, someone to talk it through with us."

Jake placed his hands on his hips. "If we're actually right about this, though, I don't think we'll get straight answers."

"We'll skew our questions a little. Make whomever it is we talk to feel like we already know what the big secret is; we just don't wanna say it. Scare 'em without giving anything away. People usually crumble when they think it's either a confessional or the slammer."

"I don't know—"

"Trust me. I already have someone we can ask."

***

Parker showed up to Dr. Ang's house unannounced. Jake mildly protested the bold move, but there wasn't exactly an alternative. With the entire town disconnected, it wasn't like Parker could call the doctor up and ask if now was a good time. She couldn't book an appointment at the clinic, either, for they had suffered the same fate as the hospital, and all their systems had been rendered moot. This wasn't a means to harass the doctor into squealing, but catching her off guard would be an advantage.

It was relatively early in the afternoon, and with nowhere to go and nothing to do, Parker was confident Dr. Ang would be within the residence, toying with a phone that had yet to be repaired. She knocked on the door brazenly, standing on the tops of her toes in order to peek through the small windows etched into the wood. Dr. Ang walked with a heavy tread over to the foyer and gazed at the couple through the peephole in her door.

Unhappy to be visited, she still opened her home to them, if only by a small fraction. She stood between Parker and the interior, a foot wedged between the frame and the door, preventing anyone from busting through. She had her arms folded, her hair was puffy from having recently been brushed, and she scowled at the girl, the unpleasant countenance not one Parker was used to confronting.

"Hi, Dr. Ang," she said cheerfully.

"Uh huh," replied the woman curtly.

"We just wanted to stop by and run a couple things by you."

"Uh huh," she repeated, her eyes narrowing.

"It's about the ransom attacks," Parker clarified. "We're going around to everyone in town, and I mean *everyone*, to get to the bottom of this."

"Can you get my phone back up?"

"Later, for sure. But that's not what today's about."

Dr. Ang reluctantly sidestepped, giving Parker and Jake room to enter. She could tell that the doctor remained to be displeased, and Parker had to be wary of her words. With the whole town as hostile as it was, now was not the time to be festering grudges between her and an important local. Especially when that local controlled her health.

Seated in the formal dining area, Dr. Ang took her place at the head of the table, glaring down the sparkling wood at Parker, who felt small in her ornate chair. Jake hesitated to put his fingers on anything—it was all so pristine—and awkwardly shuffled between the table and chair, his arms tightly pressed to his side, before sitting down. Dr. Ang folded her hands on her lap and waited for Parker to continue her evocative pronouncement.

"Well," Parker started, "we figured out what the crime was. You know, the one that the hacker was accusing everyone of committing."

"And?" stated Doctor Ang.

"We think you might have some insight for us due to your work at the clinic."

The doctor stiffened but didn't respond. She patiently waited for more phrases to better gauge what story to tell.

"The attacks started with healthcare workers. I believe you were the second person to be victimized."

"Still victimized," Dr. Ang corrected.

"Right, of course, and I'm really sorry for not fixing that sooner. Believe me, I want everyone to have their phones before the storm, but we've had to pivot our investigation. See, this crime is malpractice. Now, with systems down, I can't go to the hospital and start perusing files like I normally would, so I have to make it a little more personal. Which, again, I apologize about—I'm not trying to ruffle any feathers. I just need to hear from the people closest to the offense."

Dr. Ang's expression had taken on a sour font—puckered and tense, the direct opposite of the jovial woman Parker had been encountering her entire life. "I'm not interested in being accused of something I didn't do," she replied haughtily.

"Just so we're clear," interjected Jake, "you're not being accused of anything. You just know the healthcare system around here. And you're not the only person we've spoken to already."

"Yeah, like, no fingers have been pointed in your direction," added Parker.

"And they're not about to start," snarled Dr. Ang, who caught herself too late. Attempting to recover, she relaxed into her seat, spreading her arms across the chair rests and crossing her legs. "I just—I'm not sure of what you speak."

The sentence was clearly spoken by a flustered woman. Engaged, Parker leaned in, "How often does malpractice occur at the hospital?"

"Mistakes happen all the time," Ang scoffed. "There's a margin of error with everything, including healthcare. As for malpractice, there's no evidence of that."

"That you've seen? Or can you confirm this?"

"I can confirm it."

"Alright—do you mind coming down to the police station with us? Leave a statement?"

Dr. Ang laughed coldly. "What kind of authority do you think you have, Ms. Rose?"

"None. I just think this is pertinent to the case. The hacker is a liar, then, and we can prove it."

"It always should have been assumed they were a liar," shot back Dr. Ang. "Listen, if you're not gonna take this whole thing seriously and just play True Detective or something, I'm going to have to see you two off."

"If it's not malpractice happening at the hospital," offered Jake, "then what is it?"

"Errors."

"Errors with people's lives?" asked Parker.

Doctor Ang stood suddenly, the chair scraping against the tile floor as she pushed it forcefully back. "It's time for you to go. I will not be accosted at my home."

"We just want you to help Watson Bay," urged Parker. "Clear everyone's names."

Doctor Ang was rushing around the table, seizing Parker by the arm and then Jake and pushing them toward the exit. "It is not my concern who's names are tarnished," said Ang.

"Even yours?" Parker tried to glance at the doctor, who kept her head down as she forced the pair out the door like unruly dogs.

Once they were standing on the porch, though, banished for their bad behavior, the doctor addressed Parker's comment. "You want to take me down, Ms. Rose? What have I done to you?"

"Nothing. I thought you'd *want*—"

"Today, you want me to falsify statements as part of your little investigation. Tomorrow, you'll want prescriptions filled that I can't offer. You'll take to Google and leave bad reviews just for the sake of it. You'll want revenge, and because why? That I can't figure out. But I assume it adds up to nothing more than you being a brat and a rotten patient. Consider your file updated: Our working relationship is finished, and you will be pronounced *difficult* for all other doctors to see."

"What?" Parker tried storming back into the house, but something glowed in Dr. Ang's eyes—something that wanted the provocation to ignite a violent whim out of Parker. She backed off, albeit perfunctorily.

"You'll also no longer be welcome at the clinic, so don't try shopping for doctors there."

"You're blacklisting me?"

"Sounds like an accusation. I thought you weren't doing those?" Dr. Ang spun happily on her foot, accomplishment exuding from her square shoulders and long neck as she disappeared into her abode and slammed the door shut.

"I have a right to medical care!" Parker shouted at the long-departed doctor. "*This* is some fucking malpractice."

"Hey, hey," Jake gently said, coming up behind Parker and latching onto her waist. "Let's get out of here, alright?"

"She's trying to screw me!"

"Yes, I know. But we have a lot to discuss, and you and I both know it's not smart to do it out here."

"Fine," she acquiesced. "You're right. Let's go."

They trotted to the car and peeled out of the driveway, a heavy feeling sitting on Parker's chest as disturbing revelations came to light while she mulled over the strange conversation.

Chapter 16

"That was fucked up," Jake admitted once he was seated on Parker's couch.

She brought them both a cup of tea, grabbed a few blankets off the rocking chair she used solely for storage, and bundled up beside Jake on the sofa. They were silent on the drive over here, the sinister encounter with Dr. Ang playing through their minds like a movie. She had never seen the doctor behave in such a manner, much less excuse ignorant healthcare practices under the guise of individualism.

"It's just... when she showed me her phone and the messages from the hacker, she was so good at pretending like she had no idea what any of it meant. She had the act of an embarrassed lady down pat—like she had been practicing it or something. I mean, maybe she didn't even look at the messages. I don't know—I can't remember now. But what she said, it was—"

"Frightening," Jake interjected.

"Yeah, right? I'm not crazy?"

He shook his head. "Not at all. She totally knows what the hacker is referring to."

"Absolutely."

"Which means... which means that you were right, and these people may not be what they seem." He gazed at the floor glumly, the fights he had caused between them entering the reels of footage in his mind.

It was Parker's turn to reach out to him to do some reassuring. "It's fine. When I said Watson Bay wasn't innocent,

I wasn't expecting whatever show Dr. Ang just gave us. And we shouldn't jump to conclusions. About the kind of malpractice, I mean. It could very easily be refusing to do some tests and then catching an illness too late or something."

"That's still pretty lethal, Parker."

"I know, I know... but I'm saying this doesn't have to mean they were killing patients on the operating table. Maybe they wouldn't give people referrals to specialists to keep it all within the community."

"Do you really need billions in Bitcoin because Dr. Ang wouldn't let you see a dermatologist?"

"Acne can be very traumatic, Jake."

They stared at each other as they giggled, the moment of levity a necessary break in their morbid routine. "So, I think it's safe to say," Jake continued, "that we're probably not gonna have better luck talking to other doctors."

"Nope."

"What about the nurses? They might be willing to spill, especially if they have a bone to pick with Ang or Marshal."

Parker shrugged. "The hacker seems pretty resolute, you know? Like it was an intentional effort to keep this under wraps, which means everyone cooperated." She exhaled slowly, and then, "I'm gonna have to get back online."

"I thought you said the hacker would be watching?"

"I mean, yeah, he probably will be, but maybe he'll back off once he sees that I'm trying to get dirt on other people."

"Hm," Jake huffed as he pondered the situation. "Like you're on his side all of a sudden."

"Exactly. But, I mean, one can only hope that'll keep him at bay just long enough for me to piece the story together."

Jake sat up, rummaging around under the couch cushions, and presented Parker with one of her various computers. "Get to work, then," he ordered coyly.

She obliged, taking the device from his hands and powering up the laptop. Despite the hacker's promises to make Parker's life hell, he hadn't corrupted her software fully. She still had the freedom to roam on her device, not barricaded by a ransom message or demand for control. She followed her usual steps of infiltrating another device and found herself within Dr. Ang's network, roving through her bevy of files and emails with impunity.

Parker's heart sank while she rifled through the material she, for some reason, couldn't retrieve for the doctor, couldn't dislodge from the virus, but could peruse for her own gain. Was she no better than the hacker, allowing herself to step into people's private lives for the sake of a personal agenda? What if she found nothing? Dr. Ang was stranded electronically with an impending storm, and here Parker was, using that to her advantage to conduct a manhunt on someone who acted peculiarly, yes, but who may not be an actual threat.

She wanted to pause, to run her feelings by Jake before proceeding, but then she came across something tantalizing. Even in her deepest emotional pits, she could never talk herself out of a sumptuous reveal. There was an archive of deleted messages, most of them email correspondences between Dr. Ang and other medical staff. Notably, there was a thread with Dr. Marshal dated five years ago:

Ang,

I've got the most intolerable patients. They refuse to go away no matter how many times I tell them they're delusional. Send help.

Best,

Marshal

Parker scrolled a little further down the chair, scanning the text for names.

Marshal,

If you've given them all the advice possible, it is not your fault or responsibility what happens to them. People think doctors are miracle workers or that treatment is always available. Some of us are busy. Stay strong.

Signed,

Ang

Parker gasped as she continued to read, urging Jake to join her.

Ang,

Husband is back today demanding I do something. They are blowing this way out of proportion. Wife will live, and if she doesn't, well, that's the circle of life. What do they expect me to do? I am really quite tired of this savior mentality.

Best,

Marshal

Ang,

Wife passed away. Big whoop. Husband is demanding we cover her funeral costs, says he might even sue the hospital. LOL. I can't wait to retire.

Best,

Marshal

"That doesn't mean Dr. Ang killed the wife," mumbled Jake uncertainly, "or that she didn't report it…"

But the next email cast all their goodwill aside:

Marshal,

You should sue him back for defamation. I looked at the wife's chart. If she died, it must have been her own fault. Better yet, husband killed her. Or she offed herself—have you seen him? Whoof.

Signed,

Ang

"They were smart to not use names," Parker concluded, her mind struggling to comprehend the viciousness of the messages. "Jesus, I wonder what the wife had, though."

Jake fought to reply, his mouth agape like a fish as he sucked air in and out. "Do you think this is our guy?" he eventually asked.

Parker shrugged. "Maybe. Either way, it's kind of hard to argue that an event this traumatic wouldn't set someone on a rampage. Can't blame the guy if it is the hacker."

The screen was still ablaze with the ugly words, a vague confessional of malpractice that was treated as a joke. Even with all her utterances of potential villains in Watson Bay, it was no easier to stomach the vitriol when it did present itself. Perhaps it was a blessing in disguise that Dr. Ang no longer wanted to treat her—who knew what kind of pushback she'd receive if she approached the practitioner with a real problem. Something life-threatening. It chilled her to know that she put her faith and trust in someone who didn't give a damn about whether she lived or died. Her conditions were all a means to a paycheck.

"I guess," Parker began in an attempt to recuperate, "we should find other sources to corroborate this claim. The email says the hacker wanted justice. He obviously didn't receive it financially, so he must have gone elsewhere."

"The press?" Jake offered.

Parker bit the inside of her cheek. Watson Bay wasn't exactly brimming with journalists itching to get the latest scoop. The town was too mundane for anyone with a penchant for writing to sink their claws into something juicy. Why Parker thought there was a host of investigative work to pick through, then, if she understood the banality of the area she lived in, was another mystery she'd have to solve later.

Returning to the contents of her own desktop, Parker searched for the local newspaper online. Naturally, there was only one outlet, and it was entirely run by a sole individual. Their name was Jeffery Moore, and they had been producing stories for the *Watson Bay Gazette* for as long as Parker had been alive. She searched for buzzwords on the outdated interface, sorting through material that was neither compelling nor hard-hitting. She looked for the names of the doctors and for *healthcare* or *lawsuit*. She was only ever met with short articles about bank holidays and the seasonal changes throughout the year.

"I'm breaking in, then," Parker muttered, once again swamped by that gross feeling as she harvested data from some elderly man just trying to keep the community up-to-date on parades and local gatherings.

She easily garnered his archive, finding a slew of salacious gossip that wasn't present on the main site. Some of them detailed affairs between politicians. Others delved into the crime scene of the entire county, trying to parse through evidence with an unrestrained eye. While there was certainly more material than she had expected, only one broke the story of a man slighted by the healthcare system.

October 21st, 2019

Local woman dies after a routine checkup at the hospital, leaving behind a beloved husband. In speaking with the bereaved, he insists that his wife's death was no accident, despite what medical staff have reported. He claims the woman was neglected by doctors after complaining about lumps under her skin, especially around the neck and chest area. She was diagnosed with a minor cold that had inflamed her lymph nodes, but the husband and wife routinely returned to the hospital for further treatment.

As a reporter, it is my duty to espouse the objective facts. I have looked into this case, and I am surprised to say no evidence has come to light that aligns with the husband's tale. The coroner concluded her death was from natural causes, and her extensive chart cited no underlying diseases, causes, or foul play. She was a healthy woman, for all intents and purposes.

"This guy doesn't name anybody," Parker informed Jake. "He writes like an amateur, too, inserting his own opinions inappropriately."

"Guess we know why his paper didn't take off," Jake replied sarcastically.

"The piece is also unfinished, which would suggest that he archived it to save his own reputation—whatever that may be—than because someone threatened him."

"You can get all that from a couple paragraphs?"

"I mean, he's kept everyone anonymous. That could just be a result of the half-assed work, or maybe he was afraid of receiving some flack from the doctors. I don't know, but clearly, our hacker reached out to him first, and the journalist didn't finish the job."

"I wonder if there's an obituary for this lady," added Jake.

Parker perked up. "That's a great idea."

She returned to the news outlet website, scouring the library for obituaries. The journalist didn't seem to have a penchant for reporting on such matters; not a single person was listed, so Parker returned to Google. Punching in the date of the article and the area she was searching for, she flipped through funeral home after funeral home, hoping to come across the names of the affected couple. Nothing was ever quite right, though—no circumstance of death, no crowd that the deceased drew. Parker couldn't find anything that indicated the hacker had held a proper burial for his wife, and if he did, it didn't appear that anyone had attended.

"This guy is a ghost on all accounts," said Parker. "It could be on purpose—this was all part of the cover-up, or he himself didn't want her obituary to be published. But man—nada. And with the hospital records completely wiped, I'm not gonna be able to access them the way I did Dr. Ang's emails. So, that's another dead end. Can't verify whether or not this lady was reported to have died within the hospital or what the coroner actually wrote. We just have to go off what this journalist claims, which is not much."

Jake blew a raspberry. "I hate to see where this guy is coming from, but imagine your wife died and nobody cared? They all just pretended like they didn't see it. Like this person who mattered so much to you was an illusion this whole time. When she died, she vanished. Both of them, really. Gone."

"That's the worst part about dying, isn't it? Praying that people cared enough about you to actually mourn you. I couldn't imagine waking up in my coffin just to find that nobody showed up. Or that I wasn't close enough with anyone for a funeral to actually be put on. I've never liked to think about death, but now I really don't want to do it."

Jake laughed lightly. "Realizing you didn't have an impact, didn't make anything of yourself, right at death's door when you can't do anything about it? That shit sucks, man. I bet that would change the afterlife for you."

"You should write a poem about that," Parker offered sincerely.

"Alright, don't mock me," Jake replied.

"I'm not, I swear. It was a genuine suggestion. If you're still into that, I mean."

"Parker," he chuckled, "we didn't talk for like a week, not a few years. Yes, I still like poetry. I'm working on my *craft*—and don't you dare make fun of my word choice, either."

"I'm not, I'm not," she repeated. "I'm a changed woman, Jake. What was only a week to you was a lifetime for me."

"A lifetime?" He raised his eyebrows. "Damn, you're a lucky one; turned your attitude around right at the very end. Now you can rest easy knowing that your funeral will be flooded with people."

"Thank God," Parker joked in return. "Can I rely on you to give a speech?"

"I believe they're called *eulogies*."

Parker teasingly swatted him across the back. "You know what I mean."

He contemplated the task for a moment, then nodded. "Of course, I would."

"Great," she smiled. "I'd write you a eulogy, too."

Chapter 17

Parker: I get it.

Jake and Parker had been disturbed enough by the revelation of Dr. Marshal's cavalier attitude toward patients that they decided to appeal to the hacker's plight. It wasn't entirely a tactic, either—Parker understood why he was in a rage. Why he felt like he deserved to unleash his fury on the world. It sounded like his wife could have been saved, but the hospital was resigned to her demise. She wondered if it was more cost-effective that way, or perhaps it was as simple as Dr. Marshal wrote: He was merely too busy to care. He had his own life to worry about. So much for nobility in medicine.

Parker: I'm willing to meet up with you and talk about it.

Parker: I can help you get the story out there.

Anonymous: It's too late for that.

Parker: But maybe there are others like you. More victims.

Parker: We could help people.

Anonymous: Help Watson Bay?

Anonymous: Laughable.

She wasn't lying about that, either. She understood the mechanics of a small town. If the hacker had kicked up enough of a storm at the hospital to garner negative attention toward their practices, all it would have taken was a couple of phone calls to friends of Dr. Marshal within the police force and fire department, and lips would have been sealed. Any news that leaked about malpractice would have been swiftly denied, and paperwork would have been fudged in order to align with the story being woven by Dr. Marshal. People would do anything to protect their own kind. Parker wondered if the hacker was always a resident of Watson Bay or if their status as an outsider had contributed to their dismissal.

Parker: Well then let me help you.

Suddenly, her phone was vibrating in her palm, the hacker's anonymous cover staring at her from the vibrant screen. She held her breath, looking to Jake for confirmation, and he nodded. This was what had to happen, even if it was bordering on perilous.

"So," the hacker snarled as she accepted the call, "you think you can appeal to me with feelings? Get real, Parker."

"I'm not trying to flatter you—I've seen the evidence myself. I know what Dr. Marshal did to you and your wife."

The hacker inhaled sharply, pained by a memory that Parker had unlatched just by uttering a small phrase. "I don't talk to cops."

"You aren't. Look, I've been in Watson Bay my whole life. I know everyone and everything. I can easily push this story out, shed some light on what happened, and hopefully something comes of that."

"You know as well as I do that nothing is going to change. Nobody cares about a few slipups from the doctors. Especially not when the establishment is a cult of dishonesty and greed. Besides, you may not be a *real* cop, but you work with them on a daily basis. You're a con artist looking to make a fool out of me. Rope me in with sentimentality, and then when I'm all broken and miserable, you'll have me thrown in jail for the ransom demands. Tough shit, kid. I want my money, I want my dues, and I'm going to get it all on my own terms."

"I read the article you had written right when she died. I know what a hack job it was—the journalist didn't even believe you."

"Story of my life. My claims are too crazy and out there to be accepted just because I dare to criticize you people. What's in the air around here to breed such a vapid population? It makes me sick."

"But I'll do right by you and your wife. If you release the hospital records to me, I can publish them along with your story. People won't be able to cast doubt on you anymore or look the other way. I promise."

"So naive, Parker. Really. It's almost endearing. But they didn't care back then—I did more than just try to persuade some lousy journalist. I held a whole campaign against those monsters at the hospital. I denounced them right there in the waiting room, a crowd of people pretending not to notice me. They thought I'd fall for their little acts as if they couldn't hear my screaming and shouting. You think they're not gonna repeat that same spineless tactic? You think they won't try to silence me for showing them what cowards they are?"

"Things have changed around here," Parker flatly insisted.

She thought of Sheriff Heston, of the way people flocked to the beaches in droves in order to search for the bodies of his victims. Despite his attempt to sanctify Watson Bay, people didn't appreciate his efforts or values. They willingly turned their backs on him, allowing him to rot in prison for the ugliness he brought upon the town. If people could shun someone as integral to the community as the beloved sheriff, surely they would be able to wrap their minds around Dr.

Marshal's cruelty. The campaign to suppress the hacker's truth couldn't continue forever.

"No they haven't," the hacker snapped. "Don't give me some sob story about how vulnerable you people are. You don't care about me; why should I give a damn about you? That's the problem with society: They want everything to be all about peace and love and equality, but they don't actually want to make sacrifices toward that. They don't want to wrestle with the idea that some people's problems come before their own. It's all so selfish—the race to be the most wounded and in need of attention. I voice my concerns, and three others drown me out. You're all scared of being without your precious phones during the storm? I'm facing a life alone because your hospital decided to kill my wife. We're all suffering; I'm just choosing to prioritize mine over yours now. Does that make me a villain, huh? Am I supposed to back down to the pleading of others?"

"I never said that."

"Bullshit! You can lie and say you're innocently trying to help me all you want, but I know the reality, Parker. This is all a ruse. You think you've got me cornered; riled up. You think you're listening to my real voice, getting the real scoop, and are hoping to use it all against me. Because in the end, Rosey, you're going to protect yourself before you ever do anything for me. I am a lone wolf, and I'm fine with that. I *want* it that way."

"The only person you should be hurting is Dr. Marshal."

"Oh, piss off! Don't offer him up to me like a sacrificial pig. Especially when, at the end of the day, you're just going to use him as another trap. Entrapment! That's all this is! God, I can't keep wasting my breath on you."

The sound of his hissing transformed into the dull hum of the dial tone. Parker was left stunned, clutching the phone to her ear, which had begun to perspire. Her heart was racing, though she couldn't be sure of why. Had the hacker illuminated something for her, something that she wanted to deny? Perhaps her ulterior motives, no matter how honorable they seemed to her, were just another layer of the problem. She couldn't play both sides and expect to be the hero, and yet she couldn't fully side with the hacker despite their empathetic tribulation. She felt awful, though: torn.

"Why do I always feel more defeated after getting somewhere on this case?" Parker asked Jake, who had ushered her back to the couch and settled her while her mind whirled.

"Because it's not as simple as it seems," he replied soothingly. "I know I wanted it to be that way, too. The hacker is objectively bad, we don't need to meddle in anyone's business to restore their phones, and whoever this guy is needs to be put in jail. That's the convenient solution to all of our problems and questions. Put our heads in the sand and work."

Parker gazed at Jake, who, despite his waning attitude and energy levels, never appeared rumpled. His skin was soft and glowing, and his clothes were unwrinkled and well-tailored. He smelled like fresh laundry and soap, and though he looked like someone who put a lot of effort into maintaining this facade, Parker had come to learn that this was all natural to him. He was merely an effervescent man, untainted by the horrors of the everyday, which was something Parker had yet to master.

She sat beside him in the same sweatpants she'd been sporting for days, an old sweater with multiple grease stains pulled over her chest to mask the equally tattered T-shirt underneath, and her hair had to be piled on the top of her head in order to hide the nests of knots that had formed. This was sloppy, even for her. She was used to being below the threshold of professionalism but never dirty and fatigued. Sometimes, she wished she could prioritize herself the way Jake so obviously did, even if it was in small, innocuous ways. Perhaps that was to be her next investigation: discovering health and wellness in her mid-twenties.

"I just can't get over all the innocent people caught in the crosshairs," continued Jake.

"Some of them are innocent, yeah," Parker agreed. "But others? I mean, we didn't need the hacker to confirm what we were already guessing, which is that lots of people worked to conceal his wife's death. Willing participants or not, too many people knew about it and still turned a blind eye. I don't know... maybe the real truth is that nobody should be made to suffer, but that doesn't satisfy us. We need, like, karmic retribution in order to move on."

"Ultimately, though, we know that it's Dr. Marshal the hacker has the biggest gripe with. Dr. Ang is a little sketchy, that's for sure, but she wasn't actively treating the wife and only defended Marshal because he was a colleague."

"Are we measuring sin by how involved they were in this woman's death?"

"We kinda have to."

"I just feel like that's choosing sides, you know? Or playing God. What gives us the right to decide what people do and don't deserve punishment, and then what kind of punishment they receive? But also, what does it say about us if we side with Watson Bay and come to find out everyone was genuinely guilty? Or if we assist the hacker on his rampage, and it turns out this narrative was planted by him? I can't be sure that most of what I read hasn't been doctored."

"Well, maybe I simplified it too much again. It's not that there are people who are entirely guilty and others who are entirely innocent. Everybody had a hand in this; everyone's a little culpable, including the hacker. He can't just demand millions in Bitcoin and feel justified or hold people's safety hostage because he's suffered losses. Everyone's been through the wringer in some way..." His eyes grew vacant for a moment, a memory etching itself onto his thoughts as he spoke. Was it something he had confessed to Parker already or was there more to Jake that she had yet to unravel?

"We should probably just deal with that later," Parker said, interrupting his plummet into the crevices of his mind. "The grand scheme of it, I mean. At the end of the day, people's devices need to be restored before the storm regardless of what they've done, but Dr. Marshal has to be outed in some way. We stop the hacker, but hand him Dr. Marshal."

"He already rejected that idea."

"I don't mean like literally offer him up on a silver platter. I'm just saying that getting the internet back online and unlocking devices doesn't have to be absolution."

Parker swiveled her head around the room, evaluating the wicker baskets and plastic bins that were filled to the brim with potential materials for such a mission. However, she had her heart set on a particular item: a USB stick. Of course, the minuscule plastic was lost amongst her assortment of gadgets. She had managed to collect hundreds of wires, cords, and ports over the years, adding to her father's already inordinate amount of things. There were keyboards that didn't latch onto a single computer she owned and various disc players from a host of decades. She had broken headphones, adapters, and manuals on how to better oneself as a typist. She had more junk than treasure, and as she rummaged through the bins that had been cluttering the home for decades, she wondered if it was high time she began honestly analyzing what she had and what she needed.

"I didn't realize you were kind of a hoarder," Jake chuckled while he watched Parker manically sort through the collection.

"Learned trait from my father," she responded earnestly.

"Are all of these necessary to hacking?"

"Not at all," she admitted. "I think there's just something appealing about the *I might need that later* mentality. Being surrounded by crap is sort of a comfort. You'll never be without."

"He walked away from it pretty easily, though."

"Age makes you realize what an idiot you are. Or maybe he's started a new stash of goods and constantly thinks about how much he owns and what he's gonna do with all of it."

"You don't know?"

"Know what?"

"What your father's up to?"

Parker paused, suddenly guilty at the notion of her evasion of her parents. They were the ones who decided to ditch her, though, and it wasn't her fault she didn't want to track them down in a different part of the country. Sometimes, she felt orphaned by their disappearance, as though the only way they could shake their adult daughter off them was to run far away. Wasn't the child supposed to be the one to leave the nest? She knew they resented her for not abdicating the home—they wanted to sell it, pocket the extra money. They'd rather be rid of Parker's shelter than know their daughter was eternally safe in the world. Then again, she wasn't exactly experiencing the quiet, docile life she'd hoped for upon staying. She was rather occupied with horror and criminals who knew her exact address, wasn't she?

"I'm still mad at my parents," she finally conceded. "They just packed up one morning and told me that that was the way it was gonna be. They couldn't sit idle anymore; this wasn't the life they wanted for themselves, and I was old enough to be on my own."

"Wow, that's... harsh."

Parker sighed. "Honestly, I'm not exactly painting them in the best light. They're not wrong: I *am* an adult, and they've already done all they can for me. They settled here when my mom was pregnant with me out of convenience and stayed because I had plenty of space to be a kid. But as I got older, I knew they were itching to ditch this place. I just forced them to let me finish out high school before they could do it. We both made good on our ends of the bargain, I guess."

"But they don't reach out to you at all?"

"They do... I just ignore it more often than not."

Jake furrowed his brow. "I'd scold you, but I do the same thing... I don't have an actual reason to be mad at my parents. I just am. It's weird."

"We're doomed to be children forever, Jake."

"No... I think we're just too comfortable in our misery."

The sentiment hung over the pair, and Parker used that silence to continue her hunt. Eventually, she pulled a miniature purple stick from the hoard and plugged it into her laptop. From there, she gathered all the documents she'd read on Dr. Marshal's crime and uploaded them to the compact device. Even if the evidence could be argued or disproven, at least she could say she tried. If Dr. Marshal was a negligent physician, then she wouldn't be complicit in his maliciousness. She'd be able to enact justice her own way.

Chapter 18

Parker hadn't even noticed the green tinge to the sky. She didn't bristle at the sound of the intense wind, howling as it whipped across the forest and plummeted against the glass window panes lining her house. She didn't feel the quaking under her feet, the drafts leeching into the living room and swathing her with their frigid waves. She had known the storm was imminent, but she had lost track of her days. She wasn't following the news as religiously as she should have been, wrapped up in the drama of the case to a degree that isolated her from the goings-on of the world outside. So, when she pulled the USB from her laptop, and the entire house succumbed to the blackness of night, she gasped.

It was only when Jake and Parker were swallowed by the storm that they realized their grave mistake. They hadn't prepared for this, hadn't brought any residents back online, and now they were stranded. Ocean currents made themselves known even from their great distance, with water spraying against the glass, clouding their vision. Branches snapped, breaking from tree trunks and lashing across the ground. They were weapons now, their pointed ends jamming into the earth, cars, and power lines.

"Do you think we lost power because of the storm?" Parker asked. "Or because of the hacker?"

"You think he turned off our lights?" Jake added.

"Hopefully. And everyone else is fine."

"Let's take a look."

They slowly peeled themselves off the couch, inching toward the door, listening for the destruction surrounding them. The porch was slightly enclosed, making it the only concealed area by which they could gaze into the storm with some ease. The driveway sloped, giving them a hill to survey the area from. They had to be quick, though, for the gusts of wind could toss anything their way. This wasn't the kind of weather to expose themselves in.

Parker curled her fingers around the doorknob, which had grown cold from the icy air. She counted down in her head, preparing herself for the onslaught. The rain had started in tandem with the wind, pelting against the siding like a million bullets. It was only a matter of time before the hail started, and with the violence of the storm, the hacker would surely be able to have their way. To what end, Parker was still uncertain, but this was all the cover they needed.

Swinging open the door, both she and Jake stepped one foot across the threshold and were immediately assaulted by the storm. Parker's scalp felt like it was going to rip from her skull; she could barely keep her eyes open against the strength of the current, and debris was flying all around her, threatening to pierce her orifices. But, through the powerful gusts, Parker could tell the entire block had been engulfed by darkness. Not a single street light shone, nor was another lit window or car detectable. She could see, however, the faint lines of bodies flooding out into the street, checking the integrity of the power cables, confirming with neighbors the state of their electricity, and throwing their hands up in exasperation at their current state. Stranded—they were all stranded.

"Why are people going out?" Parker shouted in order to make herself heard over the spray of the storm.

"People are dumb, Parker! This is what the hacker counted on," Jake replied bitterly. "They're all gonna freak out and start doing stupid shit!"

Fed up with watching the people she was trying so hard to vouch for, she pulled Jake back inside the house and slammed the door shut. "It's not like power outages during a storm are novelty, but... maybe something other than a fallen tree caused this one."

"The lights did go off the second the storm became noticeable. That's suspicious. How did you think he did it, though?"

"Old school," Parker admitted. "Likely went down to the power plant, waited for an opportune moment, and rammed his car into a generator. Maybe even shot a couple bullets at it to keep his vehicle from getting destroyed. I'm sure he could have done it virtually, but not everything needs a keyboard. And based on that call earlier... he's obviously ready to up the ante on this whole ransom plot."

"Which means he's going to get his revenge tonight. This is what he's been building toward, anyway. He's got everybody cornered: sitting ducks."

"So, we have to get to Dr. Marshal first."

***

Jake drove cautiously through the winding roads, his windshield wipers working overtime, but to no avail. The path before them was a blur of sheets of rain and tumultuous winds, trees ominously teetering over the top of the car, ready to lift from the ground and squash the pair. Parker clutched onto her seat for dear life, trying not to make a peep while Jake leaned over the steering wheel, his eyes laser-focused on the battle ahead. It was going to take them triple the time to get to the downtown core and another 20 minutes or so to locate Dr. Marshal's house, which was conveniently on the other side of town from Parker.

"I appreciate you being willing to hear Dr. Marshal out," Jake croaked after several terse minutes of silence. "I know we both kind of decided he was guilty outright, but we still need to hear his side of the story. Maybe it'll differ, maybe it won't. Either way, at least we'll know whether or not we're doing the right thing."

"And if we are doin' the right thing, we'll have it recorded, too."

"Smart girl," he replied with a soft chuckle. "I never would've thought of that. Hell, if we hadn't pinned Sheriff Heston at his office with a million witnesses, I probably would've gotten that confession out of him in private and then touted my story around town like a lunatic."

"This is why you're an artist, Jake, and not a detective."

She gazed at him through the corners of her eyes, too afraid to fully remove her attention from the road. His lips had parted into a smile, and his hands weren't wrapped so tightly around the wheel anymore.

"I feel like we make a good team," said Jake.

"We do."

The storm was unrelenting, but the monotony of the sinister forest began to break. Strands of yellow split the clouds, opening up like a ray of sunshine. It was a life raft for them to cling to, illuminating the way as they navigated through the streets that had been rendered alien by the storm. However, the light that slowly splayed before them was not a miracle. In fact, the more they approached it, the more evident the true danger became.

Fire had erupted like a volcano in the middle of the town, buildings set ablaze and scorching everything around them. Cars were abandoned in the middle of the street, windows broken, and contents looted. People were running about, dodging each other like they were in a morbid game of chase. Businesses were destroyed, including the exterior of Jake's impoverished art studio. He grimaced as they passed by it, the space that was once an opportunity for change now sitting in ruin like an anchor. It weighed him down to still be attached to it, and now it was burdensome once again—broken, pillaged, and in need of repair.

"I hope they set that on fire, too," he grumbled.

"I just don't get it," Parker murmured. "Why are people doing this?"

She watched as the people she'd come to love and trust devolved into lunatics, throwing their stolen materials back through the windows of buildings they'd raided. This had nothing to do with helplessness or their phones. This wasn't a choice they were forced to make in the midst of a storm. These were opportunists at their finest, destroying what they claimed to cherish for the sake of it, high on the anonymity of the chaos. Anything they ruined could and would be chalked up to the storm, and any aggressions they'd been harvesting could be dispelled without consequence. It was like staring at a crystal ball and seeing the truth beyond people's masks—the people they were bound to become during an apocalypse.

"Because they can," Jake replied resolutely. "Fear does crazy things to people."

"Setting shit on fire?"

"It's human nature. You see it all the time in New York—give people a little bit of strife, a reason to be out on the streets, and they'll break anything. Steal whatever. It's some manic survival instinct where they feel the need to hoard what they deem valuable and obliterate the rest. Maybe it creates a sense of control. I don't know. I never really had the same impulse."

"They're rioting, though, and over what?"

"Desperation. Always brings out the worst in people."

They drove past the Time Warp, which had been unceremoniously purchased after Anthony's death and closed indefinitely. She'd wandered by it many times, peeking through boarded-up windows and pressing her ear firmly to the exterior walls, mining for clues as to whether demolition had commenced. She never saw vans parked out front or walked through clouds of sawdust. She didn't see the old furniture littering the dumpsters out back or strange men milling about, working on the elusive new business that was to take the place of the only local watering hole. The place where her feelings had been cemented for Jake.

It was the only establishment untouched by the anarchy as if the ghost of Anthony hovered too close to everyone's hearts for them to destroy his memory. At least there as that—a shred of hope, of kindness. Watson Bay wasn't completely in shambles, irredeemable by all standards. Unless they just hadn't noticed it yet and were waiting to sink their claws into the crumbling brick.

Parker was jolted from her thoughts by the banging of hands on the hood of Jake's car. He honked loudly, scaring the pedestrian who was attempting to intimidate them. Despite all of Jake's previous hesitancies, the second legitimate doom surrounded them, he was unwavering and stern. The kind of man she knew she could rely upon in any scenario, and she felt comforted beside him, even as the angry citizen tried her door handle in a last-ditch effort to command their vehicle.

"Piss off, dude!" Jake hollered.

The man wandered off, and Jake settled back into his seat, shaking his head and muttering under his breath about disrespectful people. They were finally exiting the danger zone, returning to their darkened drive through the less traveled streets. With the chaos behind them, guilt began to wash over Parker. She had driven these people to this point. She had lived in Watson Bay all her life, experienced a multitude of storm seasons, and never had she seen anything like this. It was a form of derangement, completely alien to the cityscape she had been bred into.

"This is all my fault," Parker announced glumly.

"What? No, it's not," Jake responded quickly.

"If I had just stuck to the plan... the *original* plan, and dismantled the ransomware, none of this would be happening."

"Hey, I saw how hard it's been to get a handle on this case."

"Because I kept losing sight of things! I hopped from one rabbit hole to the next, never tying up loose ends or resolving anything. I'd just get stuck and move on. And now look at everybody. They're a mess, and it's all because of me."

"You can't control how people behave, Parker. They chose to leave their houses and loot. They're putting themselves in more danger by standing around in that storm than they ever were just being without their phones."

"I don't know why I made you take it back."

"Take what back?"

"All those things you said about me straying too far from the job. You were right, Jake. I should have been more focused and worried about the morality of it all later."

"You're improving, though. I wanted to stay at your house a little longer and talk about punishment or whatever, but you forced us to table that. We had been out here."

"I learned my lesson too little too late! That's always the way with me—push things until they break, and then when I'm around to pick up the pieces, I get to pretend like things always had to be this way. Like I couldn't have stopped them by simply being a... a different person!"

"Parker," he cooed tenderly, "what's gotten into you?"

"I've accomplished nothing," she groaned. "Nothing at all."

A moment passed between them. The swelling storm seemed to dissipate, receding into the background while Jake latched onto Parker, folding her palm into his without taking his eyes off the road.

"And you always have to comfort me, too," Parker continued.

"I like doing it."

"It's not supposed to be like this. *I'm* not supposed to be like this. I don't know what happened to me. I became a wimp overnight."

"You're just going through a rough patch. We've all been there."

"Not you, Jake. You're... you're perfect."

Jake cackled, breaking the tension that had been building all evening. "Oh, God, Parker. I'm anything but."

"Don't be humble."

"I'm not being humble. I may seem all mysterious and studious because of where I come from and what I do, but it doesn't take a genius to mold some clay."

"And you're so successful—"

"For right now, maybe. But that isn't gonna last forever. People are already bored of me. Agents from back home stopped messaging. I've been out of the game for less than a year, and people are moving on. My name will be forgotten in no time."

"Not unless you make something. That's what I mean—you have this innate magnetism."

"What if I don't want to make something? What if I just want to be left alone? Start over, you know?"

"Starting over... like, in Watson Bay?"

"Probably, yeah. I'll just go be a fisherman or a barista. Something regular and quiet and uninteresting."

"What if *I* don't want to stay in Watson Bay?" Parked whispered.

Silence befell them again, but this time, the air was brimming with static. Jake narrowed his eyes, returning to his hunched-over state while he gazed out the windshield. Dr. Marshal's neighborhood was just around a particularly grim bend, and Jake used that as an opportunity to put an end to the conversation.

"I have to concentrate," he muttered.

"Okay." And she shrunk into the seat, burning with more questions than either of them had answers to.

Chapter 19

Wind threatened to topple Jake's car as they pulled into Dr. Marshal's driveway. There was only one other vehicle parked on the slab of concrete, which eased Parker's mind a little. The street was relatively empty, too, boasting a neighborhood free of destruction beyond the gusts from the storm. They gathered weapons, anyway, shoving little pocket knives into the tops of their shoes and pressing play on the recorder Parker had packed. She nervously watched the living room window for signs of life—the flicker of a candle, the passing shadow of a body in movement, but nothing arrived.

"You ready?" Jake asked, zipping up his jacket.

Hail pelted the windshield. "Ready," she replied with a deep sigh.

They sprung from the car, running with their heads down until they were under the safety of the enclosed porch. They were drenched already, their windbreakers sloshing with excess water. They stared at each other, gathering the courage to knock on the front door. Jake raised his eyebrows at Parker, and she lifted her knuckle. However, she stopped as her skin was about to brace against the wood—it was slightly ajar. Crouching forward, Parker eased her line of vision into the darkness of the crevice, trying to see what they were walking into.

"Somebody got here first," Parker whispered.

Jake steadied his flashlight in his fist, his grip enabling him to use it as a bat. He took a couple of practice swings and then nodded at Parker—it was time to go in. She bit her lip as she pushed on the weakened door, the creaks emanating from the hinges ricocheting through the quiet home. She flinched, unwittingly announcing their presence before they even got a foot across the threshold. With no choice but to charge on, though, she slipped through the crack in the door and slunk against the wall. Before her was nothing but a rack of hanging coats. Down the hall was an empty kitchen, with windows that displayed the storm in full force, and off to the left was the entrance of what was presumably the living room.

Jake tiptoed behind Parker, choosing to keep going while she clung to the wall to settle her nerves. Unwilling to be left alone, she followed closely behind him, shielding herself with the breadth of his shoulders and back. Then, they were turning into the living room, their bodies fully exposed as Jake halted in place, his arm dropping to his side. His flashlight was useless against the hacker, who had bound Dr. Marshal to a recliner, taped his mouth shut, and pressed a gun to his forehead.

"Put the weapon down," Jake commanded sharply.

The hacker was facing the duo, his clothes black and unassuming, his skin weary and drooping. His blue eyes permeated the void of night, shining out like those of a hungry wolf. Jake clicked his flashlight on, and the hacker's entire countenance came into view. He looked as menacing as he sounded, with his hair sprawling in every direction, the strands dry and discolored. He smiled into Jake's beam, his teeth glistening as he revealed a mouth full of silver and gold. His lips were cracked and bleeding, his eyebrows as wild as his mane, and his build, though average, looked agile enough to fight his way out of this situation.

"You got me," he chortled, the barrel of his gun unwavering as he pushed it harder into Dr. Marshal's skin. Blood dripped from the doctor's forehead—he had split skin all across his face. He'd already taken a beating. "Is this some sort of citizen's arrest?"

"It is," Jake confirmed. Parker tried not to flush at the pronouncement, not wanting to reveal the looseness of this plan.

"Oh, no," the hacker fake whimpered, "I'm so scared. Please don't send me to jail, handsome young fellow."

"Drop the gun and step away from Dr. Marshal."

The hacker sighed, growing tired of the charade he'd started. "Look, kid, I'm actually glad you came. This man"—he motioned to Dr. Marshal with his pistol—"killed my wife. My name is George Bundt. My beautiful wife was Iris, and she died at age sixty-two because this crook didn't want to waste his precious minutes on her. I'm tired of living in the shadows of her death and of his tyranny. I have made my choice: This is what I want to do in order to be heard, and I don't care what becomes of me. I have nothing left to live for. This man stole it from me."

"What are you going to do with him?" Parked inquired slowly.

George shrugged. "I'm not sure, yet. Killing him doesn't feel right. There will be some unfinished business, won't there? Then again, how else is he going to understand the pain he has caused unless I put a bullet through his head?" George shook his head, his resolving cracking as he mulled over his options. Then, using his free hand, he dug around in his jacket pocket and unearthed a recorder. "Regardless, I'm going to need a confession." He clicked the recorder into gear and held it up to Dr. Marshal's still-restricted mouth. "An indisputable account of what he's done, taking full responsibility for the death of Iris Bundt."

Dr. Marshal tried to defend himself, but his cries were muffled by the unflinching tape.

"Shh," George warned, "not yet. I think these kids need to hear it from me first. Once they have the full story, then whatever lies you try to spew will be apparent. Isn't that right?" He glared at Parker and Jake for confirmation.

The force of his stare sent a shiver down Parker's spine, and the trembling that spread through her limbs was getting harder to conceal. She felt moronic, standing in the living room with her rain boots on and only a couple of pocket knives to defend herself against a bullet. Though she was recording the entire interaction, the foolishness of their dress, of their weapons, caused her to worry that perhaps things wouldn't wrap up in their favor with a neat little bow.

"I digress," George continued after both Jake and Parker's stunned silence. "Dr. Marshal had only been our physician for a couple years. We lived over in Thorton, but due to budget constraints, the whole town fell apart, and everyone abandoned it. It's pretty much a ghost town now, so me and my lovely Iris moved just outside the limits of Watson Bay. To say that Dr. Marshal took us on as patients reluctantly would be an understatement—he was irate to have been handed the short end of the stick. We were outsiders without insurance, and worst of all, my wife's health was genuinely deteriorating.

"And believe me, Dr. Marshal here knew all about it. He was the one who identified the lumps in her neck as cancerous cells. They were spreading, too—she had a new one every time we visited. He'd groan and wince at the sight of them but then tell us they were nothing more than a cosmetic issue. He wasn't going to do free work on my aging wife's body because, as he said, she'd never be attractive again, so what was the point?

"Chemotherapy was the point, which was something we were told not to fuss about. It wasn't necessary; she could simply pull through. You know... I've never heard of cancer going away on its own, so I have to assume that Dr. Marshal here didn't want to run the risk of not receiving his payday for the chemo. What, we were going to dine and dash at the hospital?

"As Iris's health worsened, traveling out the county for care was no longer an option. So we kept returning to the hospital, begging for other doctors to take us on, to believe us, but Dr. Marshal had written up quite the scathing file. We were deemed too difficult to treat—apparently, not wanting to die of cancer makes you a nuisance to the medical staff. We sat in the lobby anyway, hoping someone would take pity on us and get Iris the chemo she needed. We were wrong.

"She was only given a bed after her coughing and hacking became too obnoxious for the other patients, and though we pleaded with every nurse to reevaluate her chart and have her recommended for treatment, she was denied anything more than an overnight stay. Iris died on a hospital bed, ignored and maligned. And when they were moving her body to the morgue, you know what they said to me? 'It's a shame what old age does to our loved ones. It won't be long before your time is up, too.' As if that should have been a comfort.

"Lo and behold, her death was ruled natural. I didn't have the money to arrange a proper burial, so Iris is cremated and sitting on my mantel. She shouldn't be in an urn, though, she should be living out the rest of her days by my side. I tried to seek financial restitution for this heinous act of malpractice, but it seemed like everybody agreed with Dr. Marshal—cancer was as natural a thing as passing in her sleep. The police wouldn't listen, neither would the city council. Everyone pretended like Iris never existed and like I was a lunatic for suggesting otherwise. I hadn't made up the last forty years of my life..."

George's eyes fluttered to the ceiling; his chin lifted as though he were communing with his late wife in heaven. He took a deep breath and returned his attention to Dr. Marshal. "So, Doctor, tell me again how nothing was wrong with Iris Bundt." George moved to rip the tape off his mouth when the sound of approaching tires silenced him.

Red and blue lights filtered through the open windows, threatening to illuminate the troubling scene inside. George was frozen, watching the police cruiser steadily creep up the driveway. The sirens were off, meaning the officer within the vehicle wasn't responding to an emergency call.

"They don't know I'm here," George muttered as if reading Parker's train of thought. "Nobody could have possibly called them."

Dr. Marshal was flailing in his seat, struggling to move from within the confines of his bondage. Strangled noises barely emitted out from underneath the tape across his lips, and the recliner he was strapped to was much too large for him to wriggle in any meaningful way.

"Can it," George ordered, his eyes darting around the room. "You"—he nodded at Parker—"come with me."

Before she could protest, he had bounded over to her, wrenching an arm behind her back and aiming the gun at the base of her skull. Jake lunged at George but was stopped by the clicking of the safety being rotated off.

"Watch it, pretty boy," George sneered. "I have nothing to lose."

He tapped Parker on the ankle and inched her toward the still-agape door. He slipped into the shadows, his gun continuously pointed at Parker, and urged her to answer the policeman when he arrived. Parker could see a young man approaching the house—he was alone, his gun was holstered, and he was soaked from the storm. When he stepped closer to the entrance, his blond hair became visible in the moonlight, and Parker recognized Paul instantly.

"And don't get any ideas," George added. "Just pretend like everything's alright."

Parker wasn't sure how she could. Her palms were slick with sweat, her breathing was shallow and ragged, and she was so shocked by the whole evening that she had hardly time to think. Her brain was clogged with dread, her unease nameless and yet directly correlated to the bullet with her name on it. She had to get out of this somehow, and she'd prefer it if it wasn't in a casket. If only she could communicate with Paul covertly... If only he would understand it if she tried.

"Ms. Rose?" Paul's image had devoured the outside world, hiding the brunt of the storm behind his stocky frame. He leaned his face in closer, the darkness becoming harder to manage as Parker was erased by the shadow he cast. He wouldn't be able to see the glint of the barrel if he continued to loom in the doorway.

"Paul," Parker breathed oddly.

"What are you doing here? Ain't this Doc Marshal's house?"

"Yes! Um... we're here... investigating." Cool metal prodded her. "I mean, hanging out."

"Is he alright?"

"Of course."

"Can I talk to him?"

"Uh, no, he's on some... medication."

Paul fiddled with his posture as he chewed on Parker's words. "That don't sound too good, Ms. Rose."

"He'll be fine. We're looking after him."

"A doctor needing help... well, ain't that something."

Parker gave a stilted laugh. "What are you doing here, Paul?"

"Patrolling the area," he replied placidly, as though he had forgotten everything Parker had said and was pleased to discuss himself for a moment. "The power outage has got folks all riled up—I'm helping the fellas do the rounds to make sure everyone's good. Don't want people getting stranded out here in the storm."

"That's so noble of you."

"If I could just see Doc Marshal, I'll be on my way."

"You don't trust me?"

Paul chuckled, a red flush coloring his cheeks. "I trust you with all sorts of stuff, but nothin' medical, ma'am. Don't be so surprised by that."

"You should really trust me, Paul."

"Do you have something to hide, Ms. Rose?" The geniality he usually displayed had vanished, and Parker saw his hand flit toward his revolver.

"I'd never hide anything from you."

But then George was pulling the door open, his gun ready to fire. He pushed Parker down in the process, suddenly bored of using her life as a bartering tool. Parker tripped while trying to keep her balance, and the men engaged in a violent wrestle and knocked her. Neither of them had been quick enough to fire, and by the time George had Paul in the perfect position, the policeman was already in action. All three of them were on the floor, with Jake jumping into the pile. First, he retrieved Parker out from under the weight of the tussling men. Then, he was engaged in the fight, disarming them and handing Parker one of the guns.

It was then that George conceded his rage, his mission, a lost cause. He was outnumbered. Jake aimed George's pistol at the defeated man, and Paul used the defeat to pin George to the ground, roughly pinning his hands behind his back and cuffing him. "You're under arrest, Sir," Paul announced.

George thrashed feebly, the venom in his veins nothing more than a faint memory of the vengeful man he had tried to be. Jake followed Paul out to the police cruiser, keeping the gun locked on George until he was safely in the backseat of the car, cuffed and barred. George didn't protest, didn't claim there to be some kind of horrible mistake. Instead, he accepted his fate, and Parker had to think he'd done it on purpose. He said it himself: What more was he supposed to do? He'd turned off everyone's devices, he'd rid them all of power, and he'd wrangled the man who knowingly allowed his wife to wither and perish. He could have killed him for revenge, or taken the confession to the police. But then what? He would still be without Iris. Nothing was going to undo that degree of pain, not even justice.

Parker almost pitied him as she watched his demeanor. Such an elaborate plan with no finale—a waste of his life. What was left of it, anyway? And now he'd be rotting in prison while Dr. Marshal got to tout the tale of how he narrowly escaped the clutches of a deranged criminal. *Unless*, she thought, and tore back into the house. She scoured the dark floor for the contents of George's pockets and located the recorder at the end of the hall, having been tossed in the chaos. She removed her own device and rushed out of the house to catch Paul before he drove away.

"Here!" she shouted, her hand outstretched with the evidence.

Paul stared at her with confusion. "Look, I don't know what's going on, but I'll get the full story from you later, Rose."

"No! Not good enough. Just... just take these recorders right now and arrest Dr. Marshal while you're at it, too."

Paul scoffed. "I can't do that."

"These have everything you need to build a case against both of them. And this, too..." She dug the USB out of her pocket. "Dr. Marshal is just as bad as George. I promise you won't regret taking him in. You can deal with the consequences later."

Paul gazed between Jake and Parker, unsure what to believe. "You should listen to her," Jake urged. "Nobody should be walking free."

Paul accepted the electronics warily. "I swear to God, Rose, if I lose my job over this, I'm going to take you down with me."

"You can sleep on my couch until you get back on your feet," she vowed.

Paul whistled while he thought but eventually made his way back into the home. Parker and Jake stood nervously by the cruiser, their lungs aching for air until Paul reappeared with Dr. Marshal in cuffs, the tape limply hanging from his mouth.

"I don't know what these *criminals* told you, but they all broke into my house and tried to kill me!" Dr. Marshal shrieked.

"Yeah, yeah," Paul mused, "we'll see what the judge has to say about that."

Within minutes, Parker and Jake were deserted on the driveway, the storm still raining down on them. It didn't bother her so much anymore. She was almost relieved to be soaked through, the rushing water cleansing her of everything she'd done that evening. She had sent two men away in cuffs—that was better than watching the whole town implode for no reason.

"Let's get going," Parker finally said, grabbing Jake by the hand the way he had tugged hers so many times before.

He bore his feet into the earth, forcing Parker to face him. "You almost died."

"I know."

"I'm so glad you didn't."

And then he drew her near, her chest colliding with his as he wrapped his free hand around the base of her neck. He leaned down to kiss her—something brief yet tender. The waves parted for their lips to meet, and for a moment, they were sheltered from the storm.

Chapter 20

"You owe me a favor, George," Parker demanded.

The wearied man was sitting on the floor of the holding cell, his clothes still damp from the storm. He didn't look up when she addressed him, his eyes fixed on the blank wall before him. It was a cold, dank prison—the only seating was a bench along the furthest wall and right beside the toilet, which was facing out toward the hall. It was certainly a humiliating predicament to find himself in, yet George wasn't gnashing his teeth and declaring himself innocent. Parker had found out from Paul that he went into the station willingly, and once he was read his rights, did not ask for a lawyer, did not ask to make any outside calls once the power had been restored, and agreed to whatever punishment he was given.

Dr. Marshal, on the other hand, had kicked up a storm. He was decrying the establishment, blaming Parker for his current state, and lamenting that it was her fault he couldn't procure a lawyer, for she hadn't fixed any of the broken devices in the area. He accused her of colluding with George, but Paul assured her they weren't taking his rants to heart, for they had listened to the tapes Parker provided, and while they couldn't view the USB just yet, they were already compelled by the compiled material. Certainly, Dr. Marshal wasn't as innocent as he proclaimed.

It had been two days since the storm, and electricity had finally been restored. Emergency authorities arrived at the scene once the wind had settled and repaired the damage George had caused. As suspected, he used brute force rather than a complex computer hack—bullet casings were found at the scene and matched to his slew of weaponry. His truck had been parked several blocks away from Dr. Marshal's house and contained several different kinds of ammunition and guns. George had admitted to everything without even glancing at the pictures of his belongings they presented to him.

Now, it was time for George to do one last act of reckoning: He had to help Parker get Watson Bay back online. She came armed with her laptop, fully charged and ready to be coached through the code. She sat on the ground on the other side of the bars, booting up her computer while waiting for his response. He didn't flinch at her arrival, nor did he seem eager to get the job done.

"I put Dr. Marshal behind bars for you," she reminded him. "This is the least you could do."

George eventually sighed. "You already know how to do it, girl."

"Enough—I've been trying for weeks, and I haven't gotten anywhere. Just walk me through it, George."

"I watched you try, don't worry. You almost had it. I'm sure if so much hadn't been going on around you that you would have figured it out. These people are so needy. It's draining."

"Come on, George," she pleaded.

He scooted closer to her, motioning for her to show him her screen. And then he gave her the commands, earnestly coaching her as she slowly restored functionality to the town. He was right about one thing: Once he spelled it out for her, it all made sense. She was tempted to berate herself for having been so foolish, overlooking vital directives she was familiar with upon recollection. But it was weirdly reassuring to have

George tell her she was close, that she perhaps didn't need his help at all in order to suss out the answers. Once again, it was her self-destructive tendencies that got in the way, but she couldn't go back and change that. Everything was alright; everyone was alive. That was more than enough for today.

"What was that house, by the way?" she asked George. "With the computer?"

"I told you my story—Thorton decayed, but I couldn't let go of our house."

"So you live there?"

"No, but I used to."

Parker was packing up her things, and George had retreated to the dimmest corner of the holding cell. The dejection was palpable, and once again, Parker found herself sympathizing with the man. "I'm going to leak everything on Dr. Marshal," she told him.

"Oh?" was all he could muster.

"Once Paul finishes up with the recordings and my USB, I'm gonna put it all online. He might get away with it legally, but I'll make sure he doesn't socially."

"Hm... that's an interesting twist. The mouse saves the cat."

"More like helps the cat. I may not agree with your tactics, but it sounds like your wife would have been alive if it wasn't for Dr. Marshal's negligence. He's just as much of a criminal as you are. Maybe even more."

"Well, I'm glad somebody sees it that way."

***

Parker's finger hovered over the key, the contents of Dr. Marshal's crime staring back at her longingly. His trial had already come and gone, the evidence amassed enough to convict him of manslaughter, but the public wasn't convinced of his wrongdoing. Campaigns were forged, and people rallied outside the courthouse, demanding to set the innocent doctor free. Despite a guilty verdict, they were adamant that it was all a misunderstanding—he could never be capable of such heinous deeds. People came forward with their sob stories about his kindness and patience, drowning out the voices of those who were more skeptical of his facade. There were murmurs of similar mistreatment, but as always with small towns, the dissidence was suppressed by the loudest few. And the loudest were in Dr. Marshal's favor.

So, Parker compiled the data: She uploaded the recordings, the emails, even the ones that threw Dr. Ang under the bus, and she neatly arranged them in a file that would be sent to every individual in the county. Sure, she'd be using some of the hacker's tricks in order to disseminate the intel, but it was a necessary feat. She knew people wouldn't listen if she climbed atop a podium and read them the facts; they had to see it for themselves.

"You're doing the right thing," Jake assured her.

He sat beside her on the couch, the view from his windows a serene sunset. The ocean had steadied, the waves no longer pounding against the terrain but gently folding over themselves in the distance. She saw the white caps that bubbled without fury and felt tranquility wash over her. She was doing the right thing. Everyone would see that eventually. She had made an oath to George, and even though he wasn't the kind of man she wanted to align with, he was owed this equity.

He was sent to prison, too, though that wasn't as shocking as Dr. Marshal's trial. He went without resistance—he didn't defend himself, receive council, or plead differently. He accepted the charges, which were lighter than Dr. Marshal's, and the commotion around his deed had settled exponentially. People had long forgotten about his attacks with their focus squarely on the accusations waged against Dr. Marshal, but after having visited George at his relatively tame jail cell, she was certain he was okay with what he had done and how things had unfolded. Regardless of what everyone else thought, Dr. Marshal was tied to the death of his wife on paper, and he could go to the grave knowing that there was an indisputable record of her abuse.

"Here it goes," Parker mumbled. Her finger dipped, stroking the keyboard until she finally found the courage to slam down on the enter button.

She flinched, the sound of hundreds of phones lighting up with her message echoing through her mind like a phantom chorus. She rubbed her back adoringly, quietly shutting the laptop for her so she didn't have to look at the comments from her peers as they came rushing in. She could deal with that in the morning. Or never deal with it at all—the file spoke for itself. People wanted to know what compelled the judge to rule against Dr. Marshal's innocence, and now they had it on the very devices that had been used as sacrifices for George's revenge.

Her spine tingled with his hands dancing across it. They hadn't mentioned the kiss since it happened, but they had been spending more time together. Parker hadn't left his house in days, and though it was strange to be living out of his guest bedroom, she didn't want to run the risk of ruining a good thing by talking about it. But they had been getting closer—cuddling on the couch while they settled in for the evening, sitting beside each other at the dinner table, performing errands they would have otherwise gone about alone. She could see that he was just as nervous to speak anything into existence, always retracting his hand after it had been in contact with her body for too long. But tonight, he didn't pull away. He stayed with her, holding her tenderly until they both melted into each other.

"I could stay like this forever," he whispered, his eyes glossy as he routinely opened and closed them.

"Me too," Parker admitted. "I like it here with you."

"When you asked me if I'd stay in Watson Bay without you in it?"

"Yeah?" She looked at him expectantly. Her heart sank into her stomach—what if he broke her spirit, right here and now? What if she was finally getting the answer to the question that had been sitting on both of their tongues for days but had yet to be uttered because she wouldn't take it nicely? What if he was the one who wanted to flee Watson Bay first and, worst of all, without her?

"I'd like for me to say no."

"Then say it." Halfway to relief. She wet the inside of her mouth, a sudden dry spell having hit her in the middle of their conversation.

He shook his head, a coy grin spread across his perfect lips. "We'll have to go on a proper date first."

"Oh, wow. Someone's playing hard to get." She relinquished the tension from her shoulders.

"Hey, I know my worth."

"And if I say no to this date?"

He shrugged. "Then, I won't be leaving. I can't follow a girl around the country without at least a promise ring on my finger."

Parker laughed. "Because you have *so* many prospects around here."

"I already told you: fisherman or barista."

Parker sucked in a sharp breath. "I don't know—I think the café was one of the fallen soldiers of the riot."

"Well, I'll just build my own, I guess. Are you trying to squash my dreams, Parker Rose?"

"No, I just want you to be realistic."

"How's this for realistic: You and me out on the town Friday night. Well... a couple towns over."

"Dinner on the waterfront?"

He winced. "But it's so cold, Parker."

"I don't know, I kind of like the beach the best in the winter. And there's this great spot down the coast. Most people close up shop during the cooler months, but they're always open. Usually, only a few customers in there. Anyway, we could get some seafood."

"Some wine?"

She blushed. "Some wine, yes."

"And then what?"

"I thought *you* were supposed to plan the date."

"The only good ideas I have are the ones I create with you."

"And I do my best work when I'm with you."

"Hm... better together."

"Yeah," Parker agreed. "Better together."

Shattered Echoes

A Town's Silent Betrayal

Thank you for reading Small Town Secrets and if you enjoyed the story of Parker and Jake please leave a review of your thoughts! Thanks Stella

Check out Shattered Echoes[1]

Secrets lay hidden in the quiet town of Cedarwood. FBI hacker Mia Conrad is thrust back into her past when a cryptic message arrives. What she uncovers details the unsolved murder of her estranged sister, Lily. Determined to uncover the truth, Mia returns to Cedarwood. Teaming up with local Detective Ethan Hayes, who has personal ties to Lily's murder. They navigate the shadows of Cedarwood, where lines between good and evil blur. As Mia delves into Lily's murder, the secrets of the town threaten the fragile trust they built. The investigation takes a sinister turn. Mia discovers a connection between Lily's murder and the unrelated deaths of locals. Exposing a hidden darkness within Cedarwood. In a heart-stopping climax, with the help of a figure from Mia's past holding the key to Lily's murder, they confront the true villain. **The shocking reveal intertwines Mia's journey of self-discovery with the unraveling of secrets. "Shattered Echoes" is not only a tale of murder but also resilience, redemption, and the unexpected.**

---

1. https://mybook.to/5tLm43w

Chapter 1

My concentration is absolute as I try to pinpoint the location of the arms dealer I have been tracking for the last few days, my sweat causing my hands to slip on the keyboard every now and again. Whoever this is, they know how to cover their tracks, but not well enough to hide from me. With each layer of their security that I breach, my excitement builds, and my determination becomes more solid, an unbreachable and ironclad wall.

As the youngest hacker to ever be recruited to the FBI, now working at the New York field office, I love this type of challenge: finding a crooked needle in a stack of needles.

Biting my lip, I attack the sixth firewall, throwing everything I have at it.

"Package for you, Conrad."

I almost leap out of my chair as the envelope thumps down next to me on the desk.

"What the hell, O'Donnell?! Did no one teach you how to knock?"

I feel the blood rush to my face from the fright as O'Donnell grins at me, leaning against the door frame of my office, looking for all the world like a cat that stole all the cream, never mind just a bowl. He knows I shut off from the world when I concentrate on my work and makes a point of pranking or frightening me at least once a week. Some field agents think they are the absolute shit while we lowly hackers, or any office worker, for that matter, are there for their entertainment.

"Whoops. Sorry, Conrad," he drawls. "The front desk asked me to drop off the envelope as the messenger said it was urgent, and I thought, why not do my favorite colleague a favor? So, here I am, helping out."

I glower at him, pushing the envelope aside.

"Thanks," I grind out past my teeth, wishing for all the world that someone would shoot him already. Not anything serious, of course, just bad enough that I could get a week or two without him in the office. Trying to calm my heart rate, I continue, "I need to get back to work if there is nothing else."

O'Donnell knows I am seeing red as he smiles at me, lazily looking about, taking his time to reply.

"Nothing else. Only stopped in for the envelope and a quick check-in." His grin widens as he pushes himself off the door frame. "Tootles, and good luck with your little project."

Prick. Maybe I should shoot him in the foot myself, even if it's just to show him that he is not God's gift to women as he so clearly believes.

Keep reading here – Check out Shattered Echoes[2]

---

2. https://mybook.to/5tLm43w

Don't miss out!

Visit the website below and you can sign up to receive emails whenever Stella Mace publishes a new book. There's no charge and no obligation.

https://books2read.com/r/B-A-KHASB-IXNPD

BOOKS 2 READ

Connecting independent readers to independent writers.